"Don't s...

"What the hell are you doing in my bed?"

Jeanne's eyes widened as Gray's words registered in her mind. "Your bed? What do you mean, your bed?"

"Are you deaf as well as crazy?" he growled. "I come back from dinner and find you in my room, in my bed, and—"

"That's impossible." Jeanne twisted beneath him. "Get off me. Do you hear me? Get off me or—"

"Nice," he said. "Pretending to turn me down this afternoon, then coming to me tonight—it makes for a neat twist."

She stared at him. "You think I—you think I set this up?" she asked slowly. "That I was waiting here for you?"

His answer was a slow, sexy smile.

SANDRA MARTON says she has always believed in the magic of storytelling and the joy of living happily ever after with that special someone. She wrote her first romance story when she was nine and fell madly in love at the age of sixteen with the man she would eventually marry. Today, after raising two sons and an assortment of four-legged creatures, Sandra and her husband live in a house on a hilltop in a quiet corner of Connecticut.

We first met Jeanne, the heroine of *Lost in a Dream,* when she helped her brother Seth sort out his relationship with Kristin in Harlequin Presents #1443 *By Dreams Betrayed.* The tables have now turned as Seth helps Jeanne find true love!

Books by Sandra Marton

SANDRA MARTON

lost in a dream

Harlequin Books

TORONTO • NEW YORK • LONDON
AMSTERDAM • PARIS • SYDNEY • HAMBURG
STOCKHOLM • ATHENS • TOKYO • MILAN
MADRID • WARSAW • BUDAPEST • AUCKLAND

Harlequin Presents first edition May 1992
ISBN 0-373-11457-5

Original hardcover edition published in 1991
by Mills & Boon Limited

LOST IN A DREAM

CHAPTER ONE

IT WAS a perfect day for a wedding. The January sky was a cloudless blue, the sun a cool winter-gold that touched the waves in Long Island Sound with the light of a million rainbows.

Yes. A perfect day for a wedding, Jeanne thought.

If only it weren't going to be hers.

The realisation hit with the brutality of a blow. She drew in her breath and struggled up in the bed, clutching the blankets to her chin.

Dear heaven. Where had that come from?

She closed her eyes and tried to banish the thought, then opened them again to stare blindly out of the encircling, multi-paned windows. The guest-room in her brother's handsome Victorian home was perched high in a rounded turret. On a morning as clear as this, you could see all the way to the distant Connecticut shore.

Jeanne took a steadying breath. Last-minute nerves, that was all it was. Marriage—marriage was a commitment that shouldn't be taken lightly. It was normal to be nervous.

'All brides are jittery,' her mother had said. Her parents had flown in from Colorado that morning, and Jeanne had been showing them some of the wedding gifts that had arrived.

'Lenox china,' she said, holding out a cup. 'Service for eight, can you imagine?'

Her mother smiled. 'Lovely, darling. Who's it from?'

Jeanne stared at the delicate cup. 'It's not me at all,' she said, ignoring the question. 'I'd be happier with pottery.'

'Well, then,' her father said pleasantly, 'you and George can exchange it, after the wedding.'

'Oh, George likes it. He wants to keep it. He...'

The cup slipped from her hands, as easily as a raindrop falling from a leaf, smashing on the Italian tiled dining-room floor, the shards scattering in a dozen different directions.

There was a silence, and then, inexplicably, tears welled in Jeanne's eyes.

'I broke it,' she whispered.

Her parents exchanged a long, eyebrows-raised stare which was enough wordless communication to send her father from the room, mumbling some excuse as he closed the door behind him, and then Maggie Lester put her arm around her daughter's shoulders and hugged her close.

'Never mind, sweetie,' she said briskly. 'It can be replaced.'

Jeanne sniffed back her tears and looked at her mother. 'I don't know what's wrong with me, Mother,' she said in an embarrassed whisper. 'I seem to be coming apart at the seams.'

'Last-minute jitters,' Maggie said. 'That's all it is. Brides are always like that as the big day gets close.'

Jeanne smiled a little. 'Were you?'

Her mother smiled, too. 'Sure.'

'Why? I mean, did you—did you have doubts?'

'Yes, I guess I did.'

Jeanne felt a quick sense of relief. 'Really? I wouldn't have thought...'

'I was worried about Seth,' Maggie said.

Jeanne blinked. 'About Seth?'

'Mmm-hmm.' Her mother smoothed the hair back from Jeanne's flushed cheek and tucked it behind her ear. 'I wondered how your brother would react to my remarrying. My first husband—Seth's father—had been gone for some time, but, still, Seth was only eight.'

Jeanne puffed out her breath. 'Oh,' she said softly. 'I see.'

But she hadn't, she thought now as she pushed back the blankets and rose from the bed. The question she'd asked hadn't been answered, but then, she hadn't asked it very clearly.

Sighing, Jeanne slipped on her robe and tied the sash around her waist. You couldn't very well spend the last days before your wedding taking a survey on how many brides wanted to back out of the ceremony at the eleventh hour.

Her mouth narrowed as she walked to the dresser and picked up her brush. Still, she thought grimly, she'd come awfully close. Just yesterday, she'd posed almost the same question to her sister-in-law as she had to her mother.

Kristin had been in the kitchen, scooping out melon balls and dropping them into an enormous plastic container.

'Hi,' she said, her pretty face easing into a smile when she looked up and saw Jeanne in the doorway.

Jeanne smiled back. 'What's all that?' she asked, nodding at the fruits stacked on the butcher-block counter and the bottle of Triple Sec that stood off to the side.

The other woman grinned. 'I told Seth it's an old family recipe, passed down from one generation of Marshall women to another.' She popped a bit of melon into her mouth, chewed, and swallowed it down. 'Truth is, it's something I read in *Good Housekeeping*. Fresh fruit, a hefty belt of booze, and whipped cream added at the last minute for good measure. How's that sound?'

'Sinful,' Jeanne said, laughing as she settled herself on a high stool opposite Kristin. 'But should you be doing all that?'

'What? Making melon balls?' Kristin made a face. 'I'm pregnant, not sick. Hand me that container of raspberries, would you? Thanks.'

'Can I help?'

'Sure. You can stem the grapes. If any of them seem too large, just cut 'em in half.'

The women worked in companionable silence for a while, and then Jeanne cleared her throat. 'Kristin? Can I ask you a question?'

'Not about cooking.' Kristin's dark brows arched. 'Your brother hasn't complained yet, but I've got to tell you I've made some ghastly mistakes. Sour cream curdles if you add it to beef stroganoff too soon,' she said, opening her eyes wide. 'Who'd have figured?'

Jeanne managed to smile. 'No, it's not about cooking. It's—it's . . .' She drew a deep breath. 'The thing is, I was wondering if you'd had any last-minute jitters before your wedding.'

Kristin laughed. 'Who had time?' she said. 'Once Seth and I found each other after we'd been apart all those months, we——'

'Well, yes, I know that. But I mean, did you—did you ever think, even for a minute, that maybe you were making a mistake?'

She lifted her head as she finished speaking and their eyes met. Kristin's smile had faded a little; she was watching the younger woman with quiet intensity.

'Is that the way you feel?'

'No,' Jeanne said quickly, 'no, of course not. I was just—I was just wondering if what Mom says is true, that all brides get nervous and——'

'Not mine.' Both women spun towards the door. Seth Richards smiled at his half-sister, and then he crossed the room and put his arm around his wife. 'Mine was so eager to get me to the altar that she threatened to drag me there if I didn't go willingly.'

Kristin laughed. 'That's not true,' she said, 'and you know it.'

She shrieked as Seth bent her back over his arm. 'Don't lie to my little sister, woman,' he said dramatically. 'Admit the truth. You were hot for my body.'

Kristin giggled. 'And look where it got me,' she said, glancing down at her belly.

Seth smiled. 'Yes,' he said softly, 'look where it got you.'

His smile faded, as did Kristin's. Jeanne watched as her sister-in-law looped her arms around her husband's neck while he drew her to him. The look that passed between them was so private that it brought a lump to Jeanne's throat. She turned away, slid from the stool and started out of the kitchen.

'Jeannie?' Kristin's voice stopped her. She turned reluctantly. They were both watching her, Kristin with a questioning smile on her face. 'Don't run off,' she said. 'I'll just send this big oaf packing, and you and I can finish our chat.'

'That's all right,' Jeanne said quickly. 'I have loads of things to do. I have to call the florist, and the caterer...'

Seth grinned. 'A small wedding, wasn't that what you said? Lord, I'd hate to see what you ladies mean by a big one.'

Somehow, she managed to smile in return. 'That's what you get for turning your house over to us for this event, big brother,' she said, and she waved cheerfully and hurried from the room.

Not that she'd felt terribly cheerful, she thought now as she drew the brush through her hair. Kristin hadn't answered the question about having last-minute doubts, not in so many words, but there hadn't been any need.

All anybody had to do was watch the way Seth and his wife looked at each other, and they knew in a minute that their love was deep and real, that it would endure, that it would be the rock on which they would build their lives...

'Jeanne?' Her mother's light knock at the door startled her. She spun towards it just as it swung open. 'Are you awake, dear?' Maggie Lester smiled as her gaze fell on her daughter. 'Good, you're up. I didn't know whether to wake you or not, but it's getting late.' She walked across the room and put her hands lightly on her daughter's shoulders. 'Kristin's planned a lovely morning. Daddy and Seth are downstairs already, waiting for us. We thought it would be nice if we all had a last quiet breakfast together.'

The condemned ate a hearty meal, Jeanne thought quickly, and she turned her head away, fearing her mother would read the apprehension in her face.

'That sounds great. Just give me a minute, and I'll be down.'

Maggie Lester nodded, then paused halfway to the door. 'How are those bridal jitters?' she said. 'All gone?'

Jeanne was grateful her back was to her mother. 'Yes,' she said brightly, 'all gone.'

'Good.' Her mother hesitated. 'You're not still thinking about Charlie, are you?'

Jeanne turned around. 'No,' she said, meeting Maggie's eyes, 'I'm not.'

'I just thought, perhaps...' Maggie cleared her throat. 'I'll tell Kristin to start the waffles, all right?'

She smiled. 'Fine.'

She held the smile until the door swung shut, and then she sank down on the edge of the bed. Her heart was racing, as if she'd just run a mile. Why hadn't she answered her mother's question truthfully? Not the question about Charlie—she'd been honest enough about that. But being jittery was different. Maybe she should have said, yes, Mom, I'm still nervous. I'm more than nervous. In fact...

Jeanne drew in her breath, then let it out slowly. In fact, what? No one had forced her into this marriage. George had proposed, and she had accepted. It was that simple.

Well, perhaps not quite that simple. She had met George at a difficult time in her life. It was just after she'd broken up with Charlie. Sighing, Jeanne lay back slowly against the pillows. Charlie, she thought.

Everyone thought Charlie had broken her heart. And he had, but not in the way they assumed.

Actually, nothing about her relationship with Charlie had been quite as it seemed. Seth knew she and Charlie had shared a flat. What he didn't know was that they had not shared a bed. But then, it was none of his business.

As for their break-up, well, it had been rough. But not because she'd still been in love with Charlie. Her mother had been wrong. What had been hard was admitting—to herself—that she'd made all the wrong choices in what had been her first bid for independence.

Leaving home had seemed the first step towards establishing herself: Jeanne had been born late in her parents' lives, which was probably why they, as well as Seth, had always been a little over-protective.

But, in retrospect, it was easy to see her mistakes. Coming East to live in the same city as her brother; becoming involved with a struggling young actor who loved himself to the exclusion of everybody else; defying Seth not because she believed in her feelings for Charlie so much as she was opposed to any advice that might have bridled her new-found freedom.

She'd made a mess of it all.

And then George had come along; responsible George, who curbed her impulsiveness; dependable George, who anchored her impetuousness; wonderful, sweet George whom she'd like forever but love never...

Jeanne's breath caught. Was it true?

'Jeannie?' Seth's voice carried clearly up the stairs. 'We're starving, little sister. Either you come down now, or, ready or not, here I come.'

She laughed at the tag-line from their childhood games of hide-and-seek.

'Coming,' she called, and she rose quickly from the bed and hurried to the door. She stopped as she passed the mirror. 'Stop being such an ass,' she whispered to her reflection, and then she opened the door and went quickly down the steps to her family.

The day passed quickly. The florist came to drape floral ropes along the stairway banisters, and then the caterer's assistants began arriving with chafing-dishes and stacks of covered containers. George phoned in mid-afternoon, and Jeanne was more short-tempered and sharp-tongued than she'd ever imagined she could be, until finally he gave a deep sigh.

'Calm down, Jeanne,' he said. 'What's wrong now?'

Something you can't ever fix, she thought, and a lump rose in her throat.

'I'm sorry, George,' she said softly. 'Really. I'm terribly sorry.'

He sighed again. 'It's OK, Jeanne. I understand. You've just got wedding-day butterflies.'

'I do not have butterflies,' she said, her voice taking on an edge. She drew a deep breath before she spoke again. 'I really am sorry,' she said. 'I just—I just want you to know that, George. You've been very sweet and dear.'

Her fiancé laughed self-consciously. 'It's always nice to know you're appreciated.'

Jeanne closed her eyes. 'Butterflies,' she said.

'Butterflies?' he repeated, bewildered. 'But you just said——'

'Goodbye, George.'

George sighed. 'Goodbye, dear. See you soon.'

Jeanne nodded as she hung up the phone. 'See you soon,' she repeated, as the receiver clicked home.

'OK, everybody.' Maggie Lester stood in the hallway, smiling. 'We're on final countdown. Two hours to showtime.'

Dressing took hardly any time at all. Jeanne had expected it to take forever—her gown was simple, as befitted a small wedding, but it had an endless line of tiny pearl buttons up the back, and her hair, which she'd let grow to shoulder-length over the autumn and winter, had to be pinned up beneath a Juliet cap of lace and pearls. The only thing that was time-consuming was her make-up. She wore little normally, only mascara to darken her gold-tipped lashes and a light stroke of translucent lipstick on her mouth.

But her skin was paler than usual today. The light scattering of freckles across her nose stood out in dark relief, and there were shadows beneath her hazel eyes, so she decided to use a more liberal hand, applying blusher to her cheeks and a light foundation to screen out the shadows. The problem was that her hand trembled each time she put it to her face, and whatever she was doing somehow didn't come out right.

When her mother knocked at the door, she was stroking the mascara wand over her lashes for the third time.

'Jeanne?' Maggie Lester stepped into the room. 'Don't tell me you're all done. I wanted to help you dress.'

Jeanne put down the mascara. 'You can,' she said, turning her back. 'There's a button undone—I couldn't reach it.'

'Mmm. Two, actually. Let me just... There! All finished. Now,' her mother said, turning her gently, 'let's see how you look.' She stared at her daughter, and then her face softened. 'Oh, baby,' she whispered, 'you're so beautiful.'

Jeanne smiled. 'Thanks to you and Daddy. This gown is lovely, Mom.'

'It's the bride, not the gown,' Maggie said. She took Jeanne's hands in hers, and her smile faded a little. 'Jeannie? Is there anything you want to talk about?'

Jeanne laughed uneasily. 'I know about the birds and the bees, if that's what you mean.'

'I'm serious, dear. Kristin and I both noticed that you seemed subdued the past couple of days. If there's something troubling you——'

'Mom?' Both women turned as Seth strode towards them. He kissed his mother's upturned cheek, and then his sister's. 'You're both gorgeous,' he said. 'Has anyone told you that lately?'

Maggie laughed. 'Not often enough.'

Seth grinned and put an arm around each of them. 'I hate to break this up, ladies, but the caterer's in the kitchen, trying to wrestle a rather large roast beef into the fridge. He wants to move the fruit salad, but I told him I thought Kristin would have his head if he did. Unfortunately, my sweet wife is in the shower, so if you would, Mom...?'

Maggie Lester clucked her tongue. 'He can't move the fruit salad, it'll taste awful if it gets warm.' She started towards the door, then stopped and turned. 'Jeannie? Will you be OK?'

'Yes,' Jeanne said quickly. 'Fine.'

Seth waved his hand. 'Go on, Mother. I'll stay and keep Jeannie company.'

Jeanne waited until the door closed, and then she cleared her throat. 'Seth?'

'Mmm?'

'I was—I was wondering... What do you think of George?'

Her half-brother frowned. 'Think of him? I like him, of course. You know that.'

Jeanne nodded. 'He is a nice man, isn't he?'

Seth drew in his breath. 'Jeannie?' She looked away at the sound of her name, and he put his hand under her chin and tilted it gently up. 'What's the matter, honey?'

She swallowed. 'I—I'm not sure,' she said. 'I——'

'Seth? Seth, where are you?' Her father's voice carried up the steps and through the closed door. 'There's a phone call for you. Oh, and George is here. He wants to give you the wedding-ring to hold until the ceremony.'

'The weighty responsibilities of being best man,' Seth said, smiling. 'OK,' he called, 'I'll be right down.' He turned to his sister. 'What were you going to say, Jeannie?'

Her mouth opened, then closed again. It was too late to say anything, she thought. Much, much too late.

'Nothing,' she said brightly.

Seth frowned. 'Are you sure?'

'Positive.' She straightened the carnation in his lapel, then patted his shoulder. 'Go on down,' she said, 'George must be nervous as a cat.'

Seth hesitated, as if he wanted to say something more, and then he took her in his arms and hugged her tight.

'I love you, Sis,' he whispered.

'I love you, too,' Jeanne said, and then he was gone.

She stood where he had left her for a few moments, and then she walked slowly to the window. Night was falling: the winter sun was sinking behind the dark Connecticut hills. Music drifted up from the living-room, faint and subdued. Well, that was appropriate. It was how she felt—faint and subdued.

She leaned her forehead against the cold glass. This wasn't the way she'd expected to feel on the day she married. She'd expected to feel excited, and happy, and—and . . .

Oh, God. This was a mistake. A terrible mistake. She wasn't in love with George and she never would be. She had chosen a man she thought she *should* choose, a man with all the right qualities, but who was all wrong for her. George would be cheated as badly as she, maybe even more. If she went through with the ceremony, she would drag him into a lie that might ruin both their lives.

What to do? Her pulse was racing. Lord, lord, what to do? Jeanne lifted her wrist and glanced at the gold and diamond watch that had been her parents' engagement gift. Less than half an hour to go. She paced across the room. If only she could talk to somebody. Her mother. Her father. Seth. Kristin.

No. That would only shift the burden. This was her life; she had messed it up, she had to bear the responsibility.

She looked at her watch again. Twenty minutes to go. Nineteen. Eighteen. The minute hand was racing around the dial like a demented greyhound. She collapsed on to the edge of the bed and folded her hands in her lap to keep them from trembling. Her eyes went to her engagement ring. George's ring, the ring that sealed their contract. It was already on her right hand, making way for the wide gold band he would slip on the fourth finger of her left hand in—her eyes flew to her watch, and her heart almost stopped beating. Fifteen minutes. In less than a quarter of an hour, she'd be Mrs George Davis. For ever and ever and...

Jeanne leaped to her feet. Her fingers flew along the tiny buttons at the back of her gown. One popped free and catapulted across the room, but she ignored it. She kicked off her shoes and stepped free of the wedding dress as she yanked the Juliet cap and veil from her head. Her jeans, sweater, and loafers were still where she'd left them earlier, and she pulled them on quickly, forcing her mind to remain blank, knowing intuitively that if she paused she would lose the courage to go on.

There was a bulky down jacket in the wardrobe. She grabbed it and yanked it on, then pulled the deep hood over her head.

I'm sorry, she thought unhappily, I'm so, so sorry, everybody.

Tears rose in her eyes as she pulled off her ring and watch and set them on the dresser. Then, with the stealth of a cat burglar, she opened the door, tiptoed to the service staircase, and fled.

A light snow was falling as she cut through the trees that stood like dark guard towers behind the house and circled towards the main road. The sun had set and the moon had not yet risen. Rocks and trees rose up before her, ebony obstructions set against the dark blue night.

Her breath puffed from her lungs as she ran, stumbling occasionally over the icy tussocked ground, brushing low-hanging tree branches from her face. A shiver raced along her spine. It was cold. Very cold. She had no gloves, and her fingers were freezing. Her face, too, she thought, burrowing deeper into the overhanging hood.

She had friends in New York, girls she'd met in Greenwich Village when her goal had been a career on the stage. One of them would put her up, at least for a couple of nights. All she had to do was thumb a ride to the train station.

By the time she fought her way to the edge of the trees, she was gasping for breath. The road, winding gently uphill, was completely deserted. Jeanne's heart sank. She'd forgotten how secluded this area was, especially on a winter's evening.

Suddenly, headlights pierced the darkness. A car! She stepped out quickly, almost losing her footing on the icy shoulder, and waved her arms over her head. The car whizzed by, horn blaring.

'Damn,' she said softly. She lifted one hand to her mouth and blew lightly on her fingers as she began jogging towards town. Someone would stop. They'd have to. No one would ignore her on a night as cold and icy as this.

A car raced past without so much as the sound of a horn and then, moments later, another, its tyres throwing up a roostertail spray of slush. Jeanne felt her desperation growing. Her absence would have been discovered by now. George and her family would be looking for her. She didn't want to confront them like this, like the fugitive she was beginning to feel. She moved back into the shelter of the trees. She had to sort things out first, then she'd be able to telephone home and explain.

Another set of headlights drilled a yellow tunnel into the blackness. Jeanne looked down the road. A car was coming, faster than it should on such an icy road, she thought—and she stepped out quickly before it could shoot past her.

Everything seemed to happen at once. Jeanne waved her arms over her head, the car's horn yowled like an enraged beast, and there was the sound of tyres grabbing desperately for purchase on the ice-shrouded surface. The car slid sideways towards her, and she leaped back, slipped, and landed hard on her bottom, watching in horror as the car spun across the road, finally coming to a dead stop on the far shoulder, its headlights pointed drunkenly into the trees.

Silence descended on the country night. Jeanne sat in the snow, stunned, as the car door was wrenched open. A figure leaped out and came racing towards her.

'Are you all right?'

The voice was male, hoarse—with a winter cold, she thought incongruously—and taut with concern. He was tall—she had to tilt her head to look at his face, although she couldn't really see it. He was bundled in a down anorak even bulkier than hers, and his hood was pulled almost over his face. It was all she had time to register before his glove-clad hands clasped her shoulders tightly and he lifted her gently to her feet.

Jeanne nodded. 'Yes,' she said breathlessly, 'I think so.'

'Are you sure?'

She took a moment to make certain, and then she nodded. 'I'm fine.'

His hands fell away from her, and all pretence at gentleness vanished.

'Good,' he snapped. 'Then I can have the pleasure of breaking your neck personally. What the hell did you think you were doing just now?'

She stared at what must have been his face, or at least into the dark place from which his angry words were coming.

'I was trying to flag you down.'

The man snorted. 'It looked more as if you were trying to commit suicide and take me with you.'

Jeanne drew herself up. 'I wasn't the one who was driving like a maniac. Anyone who thinks he can take an icy road at ninety miles an hour——'

'Madam, your idea of speed is as bad as your timing. Besides, my driving had nothing to do with what happened. It was you who came popping out of the trees——'

'I didn't pop out of anything. I stepped out, and if you hadn't been going like a bat out of hell——'

'What are you doing out here, anyway?' He lifted his bulky arm and gestured into the darkness. 'A woman, out for a stroll in the middle of the bloody night——'

'I was not out for a stroll,' she said through her teeth. 'And there's no need to get so angry.'

The man drew a deep breath. 'You're right,' he said finally. 'Stepping out that way was stupid, but I guess it wasn't an act of malice.'

If that had been an olive branch, Jeanne thought, it had been one with thorns.

'I beg your pardon,' she said coldly. 'Driving too fast was what was stupid.'

'Don't push your luck, lady,' he said in a voice more frigid than hers.

'Look, if you'd been paying any attention at all to the road, you'd...'

She swallowed. What was the matter with her? This man was the only one who'd stopped for her, never mind just how, and here she was, antagonising him when what she needed was his help.

'Yes?' He took a step towards her. 'Go on,' he said silkily, 'don't stop now. If I'd been paying any attention...'

'If—if you had, you'd have realised I—I was trying to flag you down because I need assistance.'

There was silence. He was staring at her, she was sure of that. She could feel the intensity of his gaze even though she couldn't see his face. And he was still angry, she was sure of it.

Jeanne swallowed again. 'Please,' she said, in the softest tone she could manage.

The man sighed. 'All right,' he said, 'lead me to it.'

'Lead you to...?'

'Your car,' he said patiently. 'Where did it break down? Up the road?'

He began trudging past her. 'I—I don't have a car,' she called.

He stopped and swung towards her. 'No car?'

'No.'

'But you said——'

'That I needed help. And I do. I need a lift to town.'

He stared at her. 'Are you telling me you damned near killed us both just because you want to go to the village?'

Jeanne's patience snapped under his cold sarcasm. 'Thanks for nothing,' she said, swinging away from him. 'I'll manage on my—— Hey! Hey, what are you doing?'

But she knew exactly what he was doing. His hands were clasping her shoulders like talons as he spun her towards him.

'You're more than stupid,' he growled, 'you're a selfish brat. I've a damned good mind to——'

'Let go of me,' Jeanne panted. 'You can't——'

'Ah, but I can,' he said unpleasantly. 'Although it's plain to see you never thought about that, either.'

'About what?' she said, struggling uselessly against his grasp.

'About getting into a car with a stranger. Here you are, in the middle of nowhere, flagging down God knows who, and all because you had a sudden yen to...'

He wasn't going to hurt her, she knew that. He was angry because she'd done something foolish—but, then, that was nothing new where she was concerned, was it?

All at once, the fight went out of her. The cold, the exhaustion, the turmoil of the last weeks seemed to catch up with her in that one instant, and she slumped in his hands.

'It's not like that,' she whispered, her eyes beginning to sting with tears. 'It's not like that at all.'

For a moment, there was no sound except the wind shrilling through the trees, and then the man cursed softly.

'Easy,' he said.

Jeanne sniffed back her tears. 'I'm sorry I bothered you,' she said wearily. 'Really. I didn't mean to...'

'I know you didn't.' One hand slipped from her shoulder and he dug in his pocket. 'Here,' he said.

She blinked her eyes and stared at the square of white linen in his hand. She nodded her thanks as she took it and wiped her eyes, then her nose.

'Thanks.'

'Now,' he said, 'do you want to tell me what this is all about?'

Jeanne sighed. 'It won't help.'

'How do you know?' he said softly, and she saw the white flash of his teeth in the darkness of his hood. 'Maybe it will.'

'No,' she said, shaking her head, 'no, you...'

She fell silent. Maybe it would, she thought in astonishment. There was something about him that said he could probably do anything he set his mind to.

'Try me,' he said.

For a moment, she thought he had read her mind. Jeanne's lashes lifted, and she looked up slowly. His hands were still cupping her shoulders, the pressure of his fingers gentle but insistent.

A silence settled over the road, deep as the woods that surrounded them. Her heart began to thump crazily.

Say something, she thought desperately, before—
before...

A horn blared into the quiet night, and they both
turned abruptly towards the sound. A car emerged slowly
from the darkness and moved cautiously into the glaring
headlights of the stranger's car.

With a sinking heart, Jeanne recognised George's
Buick.

She stepped back, and the stranger's hands slipped
from her shoulders.

'No,' she said softly, 'you can't help.' She drew a
steadying breath. 'I'm sorry for the trouble I've caused
you, but this has all been a mistake. I was wrong. I
shouldn't have run away.'

'Run away?'

'Yes.' She nodded towards the Buick still moving
slowly towards them. 'From—from him. I'll have to tell
him so.'

'Ah.' His voice filled with cool amusement. 'I see. You
had a tiff with your boyfriend and ran off, and I just
happen to be the lucky guy who gets caught in the
middle.'

It was easier to nod in agreement than to try and
explain.

George's car pulled to the far side of the road and
stopped. The driver's door opened, then slammed shut.
George stepped out and peered at them.

'Honey? Is that you?'

Jeanne sighed. 'Yes.'

'For God's sake, what have you been up to? Are you
all right?' He started across the road, his steps slow and
careful as he made his way over the icy surface.

'All's well that ends well, isn't that what they say?'
the stranger murmured.

Jeanne looked at him. 'Is it?' she asked, tonelessly.

'Yes. And here's something else to think about.' His
voice hardened. 'Little girls should stay out of the woods
if they don't want to be eaten by the big, bad wolf.'

Jeanne lifted her chin. 'You don't know the first thing about——'

'Honey?' George said, his breath puffing loudly as he crunched towards them. 'Who is this man?'

The stranger put his gloved hand lightly to her cheek. 'So long, Little Red Riding Hood,' he said softly. Then, with a nod to George, he turned and trotted to his car. The motor roared as he shifted into gear, and the car vanished into the night.

CHAPTER TWO

JEANNE could hear the phone ringing as she trotted up
the last flight of steps to her Greenwich Village flat. It
shrilled again as she reached the landing and paused to
catch her breath after the five-storey climb.

'OK,' she muttered, fumbling for her keys, 'OK, I'm
coming.'

She tried to unlock the door, hang on to the parcels
in her arms, and grab for the phone at the same time,
but it didn't work. Her bag slipped to the floor, dumping
an assortment of coins, tissues, and cosmetics at her feet.
Jeanne muttered something succinct and unladylike as
she bumped the door closed with her hip, dropped her
packages on the nearest chair, and snatched up the
receiver.

'Hello,' she said. 'If you're not a Broadway producer
offering me the starring role in your next play, hang up.
I have nothing to say to you.'

A man's laughter rumbled through the line. 'That's
my little sister,' Seth said, 'always ready with a diplo-
matic word. Suppose I were an agent, phoning with a
job offer?'

'Not to worry,' Jeanne said, falling on to the couch,
'this is the real world, remember? There aren't any job
offers to worry about.'

'Kristin said you were up for a part in an off-Broadway
play.'

She laughed. 'Off Broadway is right. They'll be doing
it in somebody's barn in Nebraska. Not that it matters—
I didn't get it.'

Seth sighed. 'Don't tell me any more, or I'll launch
into my "when are you going to give up this nonsense
and come to your senses?" speech.'

Jeanne grinned. "Fess up, big brother. You're going to make the speech anyway. So, how are things? Is Kristin well?'

'Fine. How else would a wife of mine be?'

Jeanne chuckled. 'Has anyone ever told you that your modesty is overwhelming?'

'Kristin,' he said, laughing softly. 'At least a dozen times a day.'

Jeanne laughed, too. Peace had been restored, at least for the moment.

'Jeannie? I saw George the other day.'

She sighed. Months had passed since that awful night, but she still felt a twinge of guilt whenever she thought of poor George.

'And? How is he?'

'Fine. He's seeing someone—it's serious, I think.'

'That's great,' she said happily. 'Wish him all the best for me, will you?'

'Will do.' There was a pause, and then Seth cleared his throat. 'Speaking of men, is there anybody special in your life?'

Jeanne sighed. It was a question her brother asked almost each time they spoke. She knew it worried him that she seemed to have removed herself from the dating scene after what had happened with George. She hadn't, though—not exactly. It was just that she was busy, what with waiting tables by night and going to auditions by day.

Besides, the men she met didn't seem terribly interesting or memorable. Sometimes, she could barely recall the face of someone she'd had dinner with the week before.

Which was, she thought, very strange, since she could recall with amazing clarity what little she knew of the man she'd met only briefly months ago, on the night she'd run from her wedding: the feel of his hands on her shoulders, the harsh voice that had suddenly become gentle, the quiet strength she had sensed. She had even begun to imagine how he must look. In her mind's eye, she saw a full mouth above a square jaw; a straight, handsome nose; eyes that were the colour of the January sky; dark hair . . .

'Jeannie?'

She blinked. 'Sorry,' she said slowly. 'I guess I was daydreaming. Did you ask me a question?'

'I asked if you were seeing anybody special?'

'Seth . . .'

'I'm not prying, Jeannie. It's just that I have an offer to make you, and if you're seeing someone, it might be more complicated.'

Jeanne sighed again. Another offer, she thought ruefully. What would it be this time? A job? An apartment? The night she'd run away from her wedding had marked the real beginning of her independence, but it seemed there was always another little skirmish to fight.

'Seth,' she said gently, 'let's not go round again, please. I appreciate your concern. But I can take care of myself.'

'So it would seem,' her brother said with surprising mildness.

'My God,' she said, rolling her eyes to the ceiling, 'I think the man just gave me a compliment!'

'Actually, I'm talking about your birthday.'

Jeanne's brows rose. 'My birthday?'

'It's not every day you turn twenty-four, you know. Kristin and I decided it was an event that merited special treatment.'

Well, she thought, relaxing, they were on safe ground now. Her birthday. She'd almost forgotten. Well, if her family wanted to give her some lovely, luxurious, absolutely useless gift, she wasn't about to turn it down. Jeanne smiled. There was a long and honourable tradition in the Lester-Richards family that birthday and Christmas gifts should never be practical.

'You're right,' she said happily. 'But you guys will have to go a long way to outdo last year's gift. Dinner at the Four Seasons, orchestra seats at——'

'How does a trip to Europe sound?'

Jeanne's mouth dropped open. 'What?'

Seth laughed. 'I said, happy birthday, little sister. You're going to Europe for three weeks.'

'This is a joke, right?'

'Not unless my travel agent has a strange sense of humour. I have your tickets right here in my hand.'

She stared at the phone as if a white rabbit were going to leap from it at any second.

'Seth, I couldn't accept something like that.'

'Give me one good reason.'

Jeanne gave a little laugh. 'Well, it's too extravagant.'

'No, it isn't,' he said firmly. 'I've had a good year, Jeannie. An extremely good year.'

He was right, she thought, there was no point in pretending otherwise. Seth's career was soaring. But still...

'There's my job to consider.'

'I doubt very much if taking three weeks off will put a dent in your professional standing as a waitress,' he said drily.

'And there's a soup commercial coming up.'

'Have you signed a contract?'

'No,' she admitted slowly. 'But my agent says he might be able to get me in to see the——'

'A week each in France, Spain and England.'

'Seth, I can't. I...' Jeanne caught her lip between her teeth. 'England?'

'Uh-huh.' Seth's voice fairly purred. 'London. My travel agent will arrange tickets for whatever West End shows you'd like to see.'

All of them, she thought giddily. Her flat was only a subway ride from Broadway. But ticket prices were far too high for someone living on a waitress's income. Sometimes, Jeanne felt like a starving man who'd been chained just out of reach of a refrigerator.

Seth seemed to sense that she was weakening. 'It would make us very happy if you'd accept our gift, Jeannie.'

'It's not that I don't want to,' she admitted. 'But . . .'

She paused, and her brother sighed.

'Look,' he said, 'there aren't any strings attached, if that's what you're thinking.'

Right on target, brother mine, she thought. That was exactly what she'd been thinking.

'I've given up trying to run your life the way I used to.'

'You meant well,' she said, stung by the chagrin in his voice.

'No, there's no need for excuses. I treated you like a kid long after you'd become an adult. If I hadn't pushed you so hard, you probably wouldn't have gotten all tied up with Charlie Halloran.'

'Seth, that's all in the past. We don't have to——'

'And I encouraged you every step of the way with George. If I hadn't been so damned pig-headed, I'd have seen that he was the wrong guy for you.'

All at once, she heard something in his tone that made her smile. 'Seth,' she said mildly, 'stop trying to make me feel sorry for you.'

'Would I do that?' he asked with exaggerated innocence.

'Absolutely.'

He chuckled. 'Kristin told me to do whatever I had to do to get you to accept our gift. You can't blame me for trying.'

'I understand. But I can't . . .'

'Well, we'll just have to go back to the drawing-board. How'd you like a car of your own?'

'In New York City? What would I do with it?'

'Mmm. Well, how about a ring or——'

'I'm not much for jewellery, you know that.'

'That's what I told Kristin, and she suggested this trip.'

'She suggested it?' Europe. Three marvellous weeks in Europe . . .

'Yeah. She said she thought you'd love it. Well, I'll tell her she was wrong.'

'She wasn't wrong. Of course I'd love it. But...'

'Just tell me what you'd prefer.'

'For goodness' sake, I can't think of anything I'd——'

'Kristin will be disappointed. She really thought you'd want to go.'

'Of course I want to go!'

There was a moment's silence, and then brother and sister began to laugh.

'Seth,' Jeanne said softly, 'you're crazy, do you know that?'

'Like a fox,' he said smugly. 'Does that mean you accept?'

Jeanne smiled. 'Just try and stop me.'

Jeanne stepped inside the red telephone booth near Westminster Abbey and pulled a crumpled piece of paper from her shoulder-bag. It was after four—well, she could only hope English offices didn't close as early as American ones did on summer Fridays. Trust Seth to set up checkpoints along the way, she thought as she fished in her purse for change. Not that he'd admitted that was what they were—he wasn't that foolish.

What he'd done, instead, was ask her if she'd do him a couple of favours while she was abroad.

'Would you mind very much calling the firm's senior counsel in Madrid?' he'd asked as they waited for her plane at the airport.

Jeanne, who had been caught up in the last-minute excitement of the trip, had nodded. 'Sure. Do you have a message for him?'

Seth had shrugged. 'No message. He and I were friends when he lived in New York. I just thought it might be nice if a voice from home sent him my regards.' He'd hesitated. 'And, when you're in Paris, could you phone and say hello to one of our former board members?'

Jeanne had frowned. 'What is all this, Seth?'

'He was a friend when I was there. But if you'd rather not...'

She had agreed, of course, and then she'd agreed to do the same for someone Seth knew in London.

'A friend,' she'd said drily.

Seth had smiled. 'More than that. Graham Caldwell and I both went to Harvard. We weren't in the same class, of course...'

'Of course,' Jeanne had said, upping Graham Caldwell's age to the same level as that of the Spaniard and the Frenchman.

'Caldwell lives in England now—has for years—and I just know he'd like...'

'...to hear a voice from home,' she'd said, and she'd given Seth a dazzling smile. 'No problem.'

Now, as she dialled Caldwell's number, Jeanne smiled to herself. She'd caught on to the ruse immediately, of course. Seth wanted to assure himself that she was all right. Somehow, it hadn't angered her; it had touched her. If three phone calls could keep him happy, she would make them.

She had already twice phoned and twice dined with grey-haired, portly gentlemen wearing three-piece suits who had, she was sure, phoned Seth to report that she looked fine, seemed well, and was having a very good time.

And she was. She was with a tour group that provided transportation and accommodations from country to country, but, once they arrived at a destination, sight-seeing was left to individual tastes.

London had been all she had dreamed of. She'd spent her days in the museums, her evenings in the theatres. In fact, she'd been so caught up that she'd almost forgotten to telephone Seth's Graham Caldwell. She'd only three days left to the trip, and...

'Mr Caldwell's office,' a pleasant voice said.

'Hello,' Jeanne said, 'my name is Jeanne Lester. I——'

It was as far as she got. The pleasant voice grew cross, as it interrupted her little speech of introduction.

'Mr Caldwell's already left, Miss Lester. He was expecting to hear from you.'

Jeanne frowned. 'Was he?'

'He'll be arriving in Warwickshire some time to-morrow. This is the number at which he can be reached.'

Caught by surprise, Jeanne scratched it down. 'Thank you,' she said, 'but——'

'Good day, Miss Lester.'

Jeanne stared at the phone, then hung it up. Apparently, she thought with a surge of annoyance, she'd been late turning up at the London checkpoint. Her head lifted as she strode across Parliament Square. Well, Caldwell's secretary could pass the word along to her boss. Subject sighted—more or less—condition excellent. She wasn't about to call the man tomorrow, or any other time, especially not in Warwickshire, wherever that might be, not when, in just a few hours, according to the car-hire agency, she'd be in Shakespeare country.

Stratford-on-Avon, she thought dreamily. Where else would an actress spend her last few days on British soil?

The rental agency handed her car keys, a map, and a brief advisory of British traffic laws. What they seemed to gloss over was how hard it was going to be to drive on the wrong side of the road.

No. Jeanne shook her head as she drove slowly along a narrow byway. Not the wrong side. The left side. It was where one was supposed to be, in Great Britain. The problem was that it was the very last place you were supposed to be back in the States. She had spent the first hour or so in white-knuckled confusion.

But it was finally easing off. Shaken after what had seemed a close encounter with a roundabout, she had pulled off the road, consulted her map, and chosen an alternative, less trafficked route towards Stratford. It had turned out to be a wise choice.

She found herself on a quiet country lane, so free of other vehicles that her tensions eased immediately. She had grown up in the shadows of the Rocky Mountains, and these open vistas of green, rolling meadow and ancient stone walls were dazzling to her eye. Every corner seemed to yield a sleepy village, where half-timbered, thatch-roofed cottages stood in graceful silence, window-boxes bowing under nodding profusions of spectacularly coloured blossoms.

At this snail-like pace, it might take forever to reach Stratford. But the timeless beauty of the English landscape seemed more important than the Bard.

Occasionally, a driver behind her grew impatient. A horn would sound in warning, and a car would whisk past. Let them, Jeanne thought. She didn't care—at least, not until the same horn intruded into the peaceful afternoon three separate times. She glanced in the mirror. A low-slung black sports car was coming up fast behind her.

'Go on,' she muttered, waving her hand, 'pass me.'

But it didn't. The sports car was so close to her bumper that it filled her mirror. She could see the driver's face. He said something—uncomplimentary, she was certain—and hit the horn again.

'Pass me, I said!' Jeanne motioned again as she glanced into the mirror, and suddenly a horn rang out just ahead. She looked up in time to see a car approaching—from the wrong side, she thought, horrified, forgetting in her confusion that everything was the reverse of what she was familiar with.

We're going to crash, she thought with an amazing calmness, and she wrenched the wheel hard to the left.

Later, she knew that the whole thing could have taken no more than a second, even though it seemed to last forever. The car pulled into the kerb, there was a thud and a bang, and the steering-wheel seemed to want to tear free of her hands. Jeanne jammed her foot on the brake, brought the car under control, pulled it as far to the left as she could manage, and shut off the engine.

She sat, trembling, as the silence drummed against her eardrums.

'Are you all right?'

It was a man's voice, coming from outside the car. Jeanne nodded.

'Yes,' she said, although her pulse was still rocketing, 'I'm fine.'

'Damned stupid thing to do,' the voice growled.

Jeanne lifted her shaking hands from the steering-wheel and looked out of the window.

'I thought I did pretty well,' she said carefully, 'when you consider that there was a car coming straight at me.'

The man snorted. 'Coming straight at you? Not bloody likely.'

She blinked. Was there something familiar about his voice? Had she heard it somewhere before?

'It's just a figure of speech,' she said, unbuckling her seatbelt and opening the door. 'What I meant was, I *thought* it was coming at me.' She stepped out into the road. 'I'm not used to driving on the wrong side of the——'

She broke off. The man standing beside her was tall, broad-shouldered, and long-legged. He was wearing mirrored sunglasses, so she couldn't see his eyes. But what she could see of his face seemed—it seemed...

'You shouldn't be on the road, if you don't know how to drive.'

Her head came up. 'I do know how to drive. I simply——'

'You don't,' he said flatly. 'I've been stuck behind you for the last five miles, and what you know about driving could be written on the head of a pin.'

An angry wash of crimson rose in Jeanne's cheeks. 'And I suppose you're an expert, right? One of those fools who becomes one with his machine, the sort who'd like to own the road.' Her eyes narrowed, and she looked past him to the racy black car parked behind her. 'So,' she said coldly, 'that's who you are. You're the damned fool who's been riding on my back bumper. If you hadn't been going ninety miles an hour...'

She blinked. Why had she said that?

Her accusation seemed to have stopped him, too. He was staring at her, his head cocked to the side.

'What did you say?'

She drew in her breath. 'I said—I said that it's your fault this happened. You caused it.'

The man's brows rose. 'Caused it?' He took a step towards her. 'Caused it?' he repeated, his mouth twisting. 'No, lady, you've got it wrong. The guy responsible for this mess is the one who gave women the right to vote and permitted them to have driving licences in the first place.'

Jeanne put her hands on her hips. 'I suppose you think a woman's place is in the kitchen,' she said coldly.

He smiled, and for the first time his gaze moved slowly over her, lingering on the quick rise and fall of her breasts.

'Not necessarily.'

Jeanne's colour deepened. His smile became a smirk, and she turned away quickly from his insolent, mirrored stare.

'Don't let me keep you from wherever it is you were going in such a God-awful rush. You didn't kill me or mutilate me; you can go on with a clear conscience.'

The man sighed. 'A bad driver, and a gracious one, too,' he said, stepping in front of her again. 'Look,' he said, whipping off his sunglasses, 'there's no sense in quarrelling. Your tyre's blown, and——' He frowned. 'What is it?'

Jeanne shook her head. 'I—nothing,' she said quickly. 'Nothing's the matter.'

But that wasn't true. She knew she'd gone pale as she looked into his face, but she couldn't help it. And it wasn't because he was good-looking, although he was. It was—it was his dark, wind-whipped hair, his straight, handsome nose, his sensual mouth, his lean, square jaw...

And his eyes. They were the bluest she had ever seen. They were the colour of the sky—the January sky...

Jeanne cleared her throat. 'Have we—is it possible we've met before?'

He smiled lazily. 'That's the one thing I like about liberated women,' he said softly. 'They don't feel any shame in using the oldest come-ons in the——' His smile twisted, became a scowl. 'Wait a minute,' he said slowly. 'Maybe—maybe...'

Jeanne blinked. 'No,' she said, with a nervous little laugh, 'no, of course we haven't.' She strode past him to the rear of the car. 'If you'll excuse me...'

'Wait a minute,' he said. 'What you just said—about our having met before.'

She tilted her head back and smiled up at him. 'It *is* the oldest line in the world, isn't it?' she said sweetly. 'What a shame you have to resort to using it.'

A muscle knotted in his jaw. He stared at her, then jammed the glasses back on his nose.

'So long, lady,' he said. 'Have a nice day.'

'I'm sure I will, just as soon as you're gone,' she said with great civility.

She wrenched open the boot. He was still standing beside the car; she could feel his eyes on her. There was, thank God, the requisite spare tyre and jack tucked inside. She heard him sigh as he watched her wrestle them out and lay them beside the car. He sighed again as she knelt beside the wheel. The hem of her white linen dress drooped gently into the dirt.

'Do you know what you're doing?' he asked finally.

Jeanne nodded. 'Yes.' A drop of sweat beaded at her hairline and trickled down her cheek. She reached up and wiped it away with her hand, and he sighed one last time as a dark smudge blossomed on her pale skin.

'OK,' he said gruffly, 'get out of my way.'

Jeanne looked up in surprise. He was scowling as he rolled back the sleeves of his pale blue shirt. Sunlight glinted on the dark hairs on his forearms.

'Don't be silly,' she said, 'you don't have to...'

'You're right, I don't.' He bent towards her and his hands closed on her shoulders. 'And I probably shouldn't. But I'm going to, just the same.'

She caught her breath as he drew her up, then put her firmly out of his path. The touch of his hands seemed so familiar. So...

Her heart galloped. No, she thought, it simply wasn't possible. She turned away and walked to a nearby elm, then sank down on the grass beneath its leafy branches.

Her body still tingled where he'd touched it. Jeanne crossed her arms over her breasts and cupped her shoulders with her hands, then watched in silence as the stranger changed her tyre in the droning heat of the summer afternoon.

CHAPTER THREE

THE sun had burned off an early morning mist, and the afternoon was growing warm, even in the shade of the elm. After a few minutes, Jeanne unfastened the top two buttons of her dress. She held the collar away from her throat, fanning it lightly until she felt a draught of cooling air against her skin. Her skirt was clinging damply to her knees, and she lifted it away as she tucked her legs under her.

The stranger was warm, too. She could see dark patches on the back of his shirt, and now and then he lifted his arm and wiped it across his forehead.

He worked with an economy of movement that fascinated her. Off with the lug nuts, jack up the car, off with the blown tyre. He handled everything—wrench, jack, tyre—as if it were weightless. Jeanne had changed a tyre herself—only once, it was true—but she still remembered the heft of the tyre and the drag of the wrench. If she'd been doing this job, she thought ruefully, she'd probably still be struggling to get off the lug nuts.

She leaned back against the tree. Funny, but in the years she'd been driving she'd never so much as run a stop sign. Now, within six months, she'd been involved in two driving mishaps. Each had ended with the driver furiously blaming her, then, in a complete turnaround, offering his help.

For a couple of seconds, she'd had the uneasy feeling that life had doubled back and was repeating itself.

Jeanne narrowed her eyes against the glare of the sun. The stranger was almost done. His shirt was soaked, clinging to him like a second skin, as did his faded denims. Long muscles rolled in his shoulders and tensed in his forearms as he tightened the lug nuts. He had a

37

masculine grace that was pleasing to watch. She wondered idly what he did for a living. Construction, maybe. Outdoor work of some kind.

Her expression grew pensive. Had her other rescuer looked anything like this beneath his bulky anorak? Her gaze swept over the man again. His skin was a honeygold, his hair thick and lightly tousled by the breeze. He was . . .

'Miss?'

Jeanne's head snapped up. He was sitting back on his haunches, looking at her.

Heat rushed to her cheeks. 'I—I'm sorry. What did you say?' She swallowed. 'I must have been daydreaming.'

A lazy smile curved across his mouth. 'Yes, you must have been.' His gaze moved slowly over her, pausing at the open buttons at her throat, then at the stretch of thigh visible where her skirt had ridden above her knees, returning finally to her face. 'Was it pleasant?'

The air suddenly seemed too thick to draw into her lungs. 'Was it . . . ?' She swallowed drily. 'I was—er—I was thinking how much longer it would have taken me to change that tyre.' She managed a smile as she got to her feet. 'Thank you.'

'You're welcome.' He rose, too, and dusted off his trousers. To her relief, he turned away and began loading things back into the boot of her car. Quickly, she closed the buttons of her dress, then smoothed down her skirt. When he turned towards her again, she was smiling politely. 'Be sure you get that tyre fixed straight away,' he said.

Jeanne nodded. 'Yes, I will.'

'The spare seems a little low on air, but you should be fine until you reach a service station.'

'All right.'

He smiled and leaned back against the car, one foot crossed over the other, and folded his arms across his chest.

'It's a good thing all this stuff was in the boot,' he said. 'Sometimes these rental cars aren't properly equipped.'

Jeanne smiled hesitantly. She wasn't in the mood for conversation; all she really wanted to do was get back in her car and drive off. There was something about this man that made her feel uneasy. But a couple of minutes of polite chit-chat was a low price to pay for his kindness.

'Boot?' she said.

'Trunk,' he said, smiling in return.

'Yes. I know. It just sounds strange when you...' She looked at him. 'You're an American, aren't you?'

'Yes.' He rolled down his sleeves and buttoned them. 'You are, too, of course.'

'Um-hmm.'

'And you're on vacation.'

'Right again. And you?'

A teasing grin lit his face. 'I'm on holiday.'

Jeanne began to relax. 'Is there a difference?' she said, smiling.

'Only in terminology. Americans go on vacation. The English go on holiday.'

Jeanne's brows rose. 'But I thought you said...?'

'I was born and brought up in the good old US of A, but I've lived here for quite some time.' Smiling, he walked towards her and held out his hand. 'The name's Gray.'

Jeanne hesitated for a fraction of a second, and then she put her hand into his.

'Hello,' she said, 'and thanks again for your help.'

'My pleasure.'

'I—I...' His hand was so warm. It was almost hot, like the sun. 'Thank you for...'

His teeth flashed whitely against his tanned skin. 'You already said that.'

'Well, I mean it.' If only he'd let go of her hand. She felt—she felt disorientated. Maybe it was the heat. Or his height. She had to tilt her head back just to—just to...

A memory danced at the edge of her conscious mind, just out of reach.

'Do you?' he asked.

Jeanne blinked, and the memory fled. 'Do I what?'

He laughed softly. 'Do you really mean all those thank-yous you keep giving me?' His fingers curled lightly around hers. His scent came to her on the breeze, a dizzying blend of sun and grass and hard-working male. It set her nerve-ends tingling.

She swallowed. 'Yes. Of course.'

'Good.' He smiled into her eyes. 'I'd hate to think you were still angry at me.'

'Angry?' She stared at him blankly, and then she gave a forced little laugh. 'No. No, of course I'm not angry. What happened was—it was just...'

'Prove it by having a drink with me.'

'A drink,' she said, parroting him foolishly. Lord, she was so flustered! And there was no reason for it. He was coming on to her, but men did that all the time. Jeanne knew she was pretty—there was no immodesty to it, it was just the luck of genetics, like being born with good teeth instead of bad. Like most pretty girls, she'd learned early to play the game men initiated, parrying with a grace that kept her safe even while it left them smiling.

But it wasn't working now. She was blushing and stammering like a schoolgirl. Maybe it was because he was still holding her hand. If only she could get it free, maybe she could begin to think straight again.

'Yes,' he said. 'There's a pub just ahead—The Swan and Rose. It's just over the rise.' He let go of her to point in the proper direction, and Jeanne pulled her hand back and tucked it into her pocket as if she were afraid he'd try and steal it away again. He turned back to her and smiled. 'I thought it might be nice to have a glass of something cool after all this hard work.'

'Oh, but I couldn't,' she said quickly.

'Why not?'

Why not, indeed? Part of her ached to accept his invitation. But her heart was making funny little skips and bounces against her ribs, giving off signals that made no sense.

Jeanne drew in her breath and stretched her lips drily against her teeth in what she hoped would appear to be a polite smile.

'Actually, I'm in a bit of a hurry. I'm on my way to——'

'Stratford-on-Avon.'

Her eyes widened. 'But how did you——?'

'It's part of the American pilgrimage. I'm not sure Customs will let you back into the States if you haven't seen Anne Hathaway's cottage.'

He laughed, and she did, too. Some of her tension drained away. 'Are tourists that predictable?'

'Yup.' He cocked his head to the side, studying her. 'Not that there's anything wrong with seeing Stratford. It's just that there are some great little places you shouldn't miss along the way.'

'Such as?'

'Such as Broadway and Barnsley and I'll tell you the names of half a dozen others over cold ale at The Swan and Rose Inn.'

It was impossible not to laugh with him again. 'It's tempting. Really. But . . .'

'We could have a lovely afternoon together.'

Jeanne's smile tilted. There was something in his voice, a hidden promise, that made her breath catch.

'I'm sure the inn's charming,' she said quickly.

His voice became soft. 'I wasn't talking about the inn.'

Suddenly, all the laughter was gone. She looked up at him, and their eyes met. Oh, lord, she thought, lord . . .

His eyes, those winter-sky eyes, had suddenly filled with heat. There was no pretending she didn't know what he wanted. What shocked her was that it was what she wanted, too. She wanted to be with him in some quiet place, to feel his arms around her as she tasted his mouth, felt the hardness of his body as he whispered his desire to her.

The realisation stunned her. Jeanne stumbled back. 'No,' she said huskily. 'No, that's impossible.'

He stepped forward and put his fingers lightly over her mouth. Her parted lips caught the faintest taste of his skin, sun-warmed and salty. It sent her pulse careering.

'Don't say no.' The words were almost a whisper. His gaze moved over her face, soft as a caress. 'At least agree to get into your car and think about it while you follow me towards the pub.'

The only possible response was 'no'. But her lips couldn't form the word. Something glinted in his eyes and his hand slipped to her cheek.

'Say you will,' he said.

'I—I ...'

His fingers curved around her chin, and he bent suddenly and kissed her mouth, hard and fast.

'Follow me,' he whispered, and then his hand fell away from her.

She watched in silence as he walked to the black sports car. He looked over at her and she turned and slipped behind the wheel of the rental car. The sports car engine roared throatily and its tyres screamed as he pulled out on to the road.

Jeanne hesitated. Then she turned the key and swung out behind him.

The pub came up quickly, just as he'd promised. It stood in lonely splendour against the blue sky, its painted sign swinging gently in the warm breeze.

The sports car slowed, its signal light blinking, and Jeanne slowed as well. Then, the black car swung into the car park beside the inn and waited. Jeanne drew in her breath, slowed almost to a crawl as she approached the driveway, then stepped hard on the accelerator and shot by.

She lifted one hand from the steering-wheel and touched it to her lips. His kiss had been swift, but she still felt the imprint of it on her mouth.

It was a good thing her trip was almost over, she thought as her car rushed through the countryside. She had done some crazy things in her life, but tumbling into bed with a man she had just met was not one of them.

But she had wanted to. Oh, she had...

A tremor shot through her. Enough, Jeanne told herself sternly. She concentrated on driving. After a while, she had almost convinced herself that she had misinterpreted the whole incident.

Mr Gray had been right about one thing, Jeanne thought hours later. There were lots of lovely places to see, which was just as well because Stratford had been something of a disappointment. The town was so jammed with tourists that she'd taken just a quick look, then driven on.

By late afternoon, Jeanne had got herself comfortably lost on a country lane that wound between fields of grazing sheep and ponies. She had planned on spending the night at a bed and breakfast back in Stratford, one that the girl at the car-hire firm had recommended, but she was sure she'd find another one. What she hoped for was a house that was old and handsome and filled with legend and romance...

Like the one ahead. She slowed the car beside the discreet B and B sign and peered down the tree-lined lane that led to the house. It looked as if it had stood in these fields forever. Chimneys rose from the slate roof, and roses climbed its stone walls.

An old man wearing overalls and dark green boots opened the door at her knock. She smiled politely.

'Good afternoon,' she said. 'Have you a room for the night?'

He shrugged his shoulders. 'It's the missus who runs this. But she's not here just now. If you want to stop back in an hour or so...'

Jeanne glanced at her watch. It was getting late. If there was no accommodation available, it was probably best to go on. With a reluctant sigh, she shook her head.

'I don't think so,' she said. 'Thank you just the same.'

'Well, let me just check the guest book.' He picked up the register, peered into it, then looked at her and smiled. 'Looks as if there's one room left.'

'Are you sure?'

He waved his hand. 'It's yours. I'll just tell the missus and you can sign in later. All right?'

It was, Jeanne thought, better than all right. It was perfect. The room was wonderful, just the kind she had imagined. There was a high four-poster bed covered in a floral fabric that matched the curtains and wallpaper. A stone fireplace faced the bed with the wood for a fire neatly laid on the hearth. The bath was not en suite, but it was only just down the hall.

Satisfied, Jeanne took one last look around, then closed the door after her and went downstairs. There was time to do a bit more sightseeing before sunset.

She returned later than she'd expected. It had been slow going, driving these narrow roads at night. A light rain was falling as she approached the house.

A hush of dark silence lay over it, except for pale pools of light at the door and on the stairs. Jeanne made her way to her room quietly, smiling a little when she opened the door and stepped inside. The room was as handsome and old-fashioned as she'd remembered.

Humming softly, she undressed and slipped on a cotton nightgown. The rain had brought a chill to the room, and she gave a wistful glance at the fireplace as she put her discarded clothing and her suitcase into the armoire. Perhaps she'd try her hand at a fire, she thought as she drew on her robe. But first she'd wash and get ready for bed.

She paused in the doorway, startled, when she returned from the bathroom. Someone had been in her room; her pulse rocketed as her gaze went rapidly from the lamp that had been lit beside the bed to the neatly turned-down blanket to the fire blazing on the hearth, and then she let out her breath.

Of course. Either her host or his wife had paid a visit.

How nice, she thought as she peeled off her robe and climbed into bed. How very nice. How...

Jeanne's eyelids fluttered closed, and she slept.

She came awake rudely, stunned into consciousness by a booming peal of thunder. Lightning lit the room, illuminating it harshly, while rain pelted the windows.

Jeanne struggled to get her bearings. She wasn't afraid of storms, but there was something disquieting about awakening to this awesome a display of nature in such strange surroundings...

The hair rose on the back of her neck. Someone was in the room. *Someone was in the room!* Oh, God! She could feel his presence, she could...

Her heart leaped into her throat as a dark shadow crossed before the fire still blazing in the hearth. It was huge, menacing, and now it was coming towards her, it was...

Her scream was swallowed in a rolling clap of thunder as a weight settled on to the bed beside her. Lightning arced across the sky, filling the room with a flickering light. Jeanne's eyes widened with terror as a face, half cast in shadow, stared down at her. She opened her mouth to scream again, but a man's hand clamped down hard across her lips.

Lightning lit his face, and she felt the sharp knife-edge of terror.

The intruder in her bedroom was the man named Gray.

Fear turned her blood cold. He had followed her here: it would have been all too simple. He could have been behind her all afternoon and she'd never have known it, the way these roads twisted and turned. Lurid headlines danced through her mind, and she fought them back. She had to get away.

Their eyes met. For a second, she thought he looked as stunned as she felt, but that was impossible. He had come after her. And she had to do something. She had to think of a way to...

She sank her teeth into his hand as hard as she could. The salty taste of his blood filtered along her tongue.

'Damn it to hell,' he said, his voice hissing into the silence. 'What do you think you're doing?'

Jeanne twisted her head, trying for better purchase. He let out a stream of curses as he tried to pull his hand free, but she only clamped her teeth harder. Gray rolled his body across hers. He was half naked; she could feel the roughness of the hair on his chest against her flesh, and the touch of his skin against hers sent a new bolt of terror shooting through her veins.

'Let go. Damn you, woman, do you hear me?'

He uttered a short, ugly word, then jammed his knee between her legs. His free hand closed around her throat.

'OK, lady,' he said grimly, his mouth almost at her ear. 'OK, we'll do this the hard way.' His fingers curled around her neck, their pressure insistent. 'Let go,' he whispered. Jeanne arched towards him in panic as the pressure increased. 'That's right,' he said, as her eyes fastened on his, 'you figured it out. If you want to breathe, you'd better get your teeth out of my hand. If you don't...'

He didn't have to say any more. His touch was rough, his message brutally clear. She would suffocate if he kept this up. Jeanne nodded, then opened her mouth and let go of his hand.

'Don't scream,' he warned her. His thumb lay in the hollow of her throat. 'Do you understand? Because if you do...'

His thumb pressed deeper for a second, and her pulse leaped against it.

'I won't scream.'

'You damn well better not.'

He was still lying above her, his hard body pinning her to the bed. In the struggle, her nightgown had ridden up, and she could feel the heat of his leg as it pressed between her thighs.

Don't let him see how frightened you are, she thought, and she forced herself to look up into his face.

'Someone's bound to have seen you come in,' she said. 'If you're wise, you'll leave now, before——'

'What the hell are you doing in my bed?'

'I won't tell anyone, if you——' Her eyes widened as his words registered in her mind. '*Your* bed? What do you mean, your bed?'

He put his injured hand to his mouth and sucked at the wound her teeth had left.

'Are you deaf as well as crazy?' he growled. 'I come back from dinner and find you in *my* room, in *my* bed, and——'

'That's impossible. This is my room, and——'

'Wait a minute,' he said softly.

Jeanne twisted beneath him. 'Get off me. Do you hear me? Get off, or——'

'Nice,' he said. A smile twisted across his mouth. 'Very nice. Pretending to turn me down this afternoon, then coming to me tonight—it makes for a neat twist.'

She stared at him. 'What?'

He shifted his weight, until she could feel every hard inch of him pressing against her.

'Hell, it was inspired.' He chuckled softly. 'Very creative.'

'You think I—you think I set this up?' she asked slowly. 'That I was waiting here for you?'

His answer was a slow, sexy smile. 'I like creativity in my women.'

Jeanne's heart kicked against her ribs. 'Are you crazy? How could I have managed that? I didn't know where you were going. And I drove off before you——'

She gasped as his hand brushed lightly across her breasts. 'What'd you do, pull off someplace, then fall in behind me?' He smiled lazily. 'I'm flattered, sweetheart. Very flattered.'

'Will you listen? I'm not——'

Her breath caught as he bent to her and his mouth touched her throat.

'What a nice surprise on a rainy evening, to find you all warm and cosy in my bed.'

Heat moved slowly through her veins, warming her flesh. Jeanne stared at him, then swallowed drily.

'Is that the story you're going to give the police when I report what's happened? Well, it won't work, Mr Gray. This is *my* room, and you broke into it.'

His brows rose. 'I see,' he said. 'And, of course, you're registered.'

'Registered?' Jeanne swallowed again. 'Of course.' Their eyes met, and she looked quickly away. 'I didn't sign anything, if that's what you mean. But the old man said——'

'I'll bet you didn't.' His voice was a purr. 'You were too busy tiptoeing up the stairs to my room.'

'Don't be ridiculous. The old man said his wife took care of things, but she wasn't around. So he said I could have this room, and... What's the matter?'

Gray was staring down at her, a puzzled expression on his face. 'It was a woman who rented the room to me,' he said slowly. 'Late this evening.'

'Well, it was her husband who rented it to me,' Jeanne said impatiently. 'This afternoon. He said he'd tell her...'

They stared at each other, and then he rolled away.

'They rented the same room to both of us,' he said, thrusting his hand into his hair and pushing it back from his forehead. 'Who would have believed it?'

Jeanne drew a deep breath. 'Not me,' she said, sitting up against the pillows.

Gray lifted the hand she'd bitten and looked at it. 'You've got a powerful set of teeth, lady.'

'I'm sorry if I hurt you,' she said coldly. 'But you must admit, you deserved it.'

He swung his head towards her. 'For what? Climbing into my own bed?'

'For assuming I—I . . .'

The dark scowl on his face gave way to a smile. 'Wishful thinking.'

Jeanne flushed as his gaze moved slowly over her, from her face to her throat to the rounded rise of her breasts beneath her nightgown. She caught the blanket in her hands and drew it to her chin.

'Mr Gray——'

'Just Gray. It's what everybody calls me.'

'*Mr* Gray,' she repeated, 'I'd appreciate it if you'd——'

'It would have been lovely, though.' He rolled on to his side, dug his elbow into the mattress, and propped his head on his hand. 'If you really had been waiting for me, I mean.'

There was laughter in his voice, but there was something else, an edge that made Jeanne's breath catch. She stared at him, then scrambled towards the edge of the bed.

'I think you'd better leave.'

He laughed softly. 'Haven't you got that wrong? This room is mine.'

She glanced out the window, at the dark, wet night. 'You wouldn't make me . . . ?'

'You're right. I wouldn't.' He sat up and smiled at her. 'Our room, then. How's that sound?'

'Don't be silly. It isn't . . .'

He moved closer, then reached out and cupped her flushed cheek in his hand.

'You can stay the night and share it.'

Jeanne's pulse leaped. Thunder rumbled far in the distance. In the dying light of the fire, Gray's face was striped in shadow.

'No.'

His other hand came up to frame her face. A tremor went through her as his fingers threaded into her hair, and suddenly the tension between them was more powerful than the storm.

'We'd be good together,' he said softly. 'You know that.'

Jeanne's heart turned over. 'Please...'

He shifted closer. 'Please, what?'

His voice was a whisper in the night. She closed her eyes as he bent to her and brushed his mouth lightly over hers.

'Please—please let go of me.'

She had meant it to be a command. But even she knew it sounded more like a plea.

'Is that what you really want me to do?' he asked as he eased her slowly down against the pillows.

'Yes,' she whispered. 'Of course. What else would I...?'

She moaned as he bent his head and pressed his open mouth to her throat.

'You're beautiful,' he murmured, drawing back and looking at her as she lay beneath him. 'So beautiful.'

Stop him, Jeanne told herself. Stop him.

But his hands were warm as they stroked her body, his mouth a flame as it coaxed a response from hers. Slowly, slowly, her hands lifted to his bare chest, her palms flattening over the thudding beat of his heart.

Her eyes fell shut as his lips moved against hers, gently at first, then with a demand that drew a whisper of pleasure from her throat.

When he drew back, she reached out to him. But he caught her wrists and held them fast.

'Tell me you want me,' he said.

A tremor went through her.

'Tell me,' he demanded. One hand fell to her breast and cupped it through the soft cotton nightgown. Her breath hissed in the silence, and a fierce look of triumph glinted in his eyes. 'Say it,' he whispered.

Jeanne stared up at him. In the shadowy, fire-lit room, he was as much dream as reality. The world was far away.

But morning would come eventually, and all that would be left would be the memory of a night spent in the arms of a stranger.

What seemed magic now would be revealed for what it really was, a tawdry combination of fantasy and desire.

Jeanne turned her face from his. 'Let me up,' she said quietly.

His body tensed against hers and she thought, for a heartbeat, that he would not. Her blood thickened at the possibility. But suddenly he uttered a short, ugly oath. In one fluid motion, he rolled away from her and off the bed.

'You're lucky this time, lady.' His voice was harsh as he stood above her, breathing heavily. 'Next time, it might be different.'

Jeanne stared at him. 'You don't understand. I——'

'That's a hell of a dangerous game you play.' Firelight danced over his naked chest and shoulders as he snatched up his clothing. He straightened and stared down at her, and she drew back at the cold rage she saw in his eyes. 'You're just damned lucky you got away without being hurt.'

'Please. I didn't mean——'

'The woods are full of wolves, and a little girl who's not careful may never make it out in one piece.'

Jeanne watched, transfixed, as Gray stalked to the door, yanked it open, then slammed it after him, and then she jumped from the bed, ran to the door and locked it.

It was time to admit the truth, she thought, leaning back against the wall.

The man in her bed tonight and the man she'd met that cold January evening were one and the same. She'd known it, in her heart, since he'd stormed out of his car this afternoon.

How could something like that happen? Coincidence was one thing, but something like this was impossible—yet not as impossible as how she had behaved only moments ago.

Jeanne put her hands to her face. What had just happened—what had almost happened—was what she had longed for since the night they'd met.

And that, she thought unhappily, was really impossible.

After a moment, she sighed, walked slowly to the bed, and sank down on it. Thank God she was leaving England in only two more days. Otherwise, the way things were going, fate would probably find a way to put the man named Gray in her path again.

And that would never do.

Her hand went to her mouth, tracing the remembered taste and touch of his.

After all, how many times could Little Red Riding Hood manage to get away safely?

CHAPTER FOUR

JEANNE awoke to bright sunshine, heart hammering, half afraid she'd somehow find the man named Gray still in her room.

But she was alone. The breath whooshed from her lungs and she sank back against the pillows in relief, wondering, for a moment, if perhaps she had dreamed it all.

It was possible, wasn't it? Dreams could be frighteningly real. When she was little, she'd once dreamed that her kitten had run away, and nothing had convinced her it hadn't until she'd held its warm, purring body tightly in her arms.

But she wasn't a child any more, she thought as she sat up and tossed the covers aside. What was the sense in pretending? What had happened in this room last night had been all too real. Gray had lain beside her, he had taken her in his arms, he had kissed her—and she—she had kissed him back.

A flush rose to her cheeks as she remembered. What a bastard the man was, taking advantage of her that way. She'd been tired and confused, and he'd capitalised on it. Biting him hadn't been enough. Why hadn't she slapped his face until his ears rang? She could have done something more. She could have...

She could have let him stay. The storm that had raged between them had been wilder than the one outside the window. She could have spent the night in his arms, she could have...

What was she thinking? Jeanne rose quickly from the bed and marched across the room. She was exhausted, that was the trouble, but who wouldn't be after tossing and turning half the night?

What she needed was coffee. Strong coffee, and lots of it. But not here, in this house—the thought of trying to explain her presence to the proprietress made her head spin. There was a little café at the crossroads, she'd noticed it yesterday. She would breakfast there, consult her map and guidebook, and go on with her tour of the Cotswolds. One unpleasant incident wasn't going to ruin the few days that remained of her vacation.

Squaring her shoulders, Jeanne finished dressing, tucked ten pounds beneath the ashtray on the bedside table, then snatched up her suitcase and let herself out of her bedroom. If she moved fast enough, she could be gone long before anyone stirred.

Bacon, eggs, and a steaming pot of coffee went a long way to clearing the cobwebs from her brain, and the beauty of the day and the countryside did the rest. Jeanne laid out her route for the day. First, she doubled back to Stratford, reaching it before the tourist hordes descended, and walked the streets of the little town in relative peace and quiet. She lunched at an ancient pub beside the Avon, happily feeding most of her sandwich to the pair of swans that sailed regally along the river's banks. By mid-afternoon she was high on the ramparts at Warwick Castle, gazing out at the surrounding landscape.

Warwick, she thought idly, Warwick—why was that name so familiar?

Of course, Seth's friend, Graham Caldwell, was in Warwickshire somewhere. Wasn't that what the dragon on the telephone had said?

Jeanne shaded her eyes. Houses, large and small, dotted the rolling green meadows. Was one of them Caldwell's? Maybe she ought to phone the man. He probably had a charming vacation home, something with a thatched roof and half-timbered walls like the ones she'd passed yesterday. It might be pleasant to visit such a place...

...And spend an endless evening with a doting, middle-aged Graham Caldwell who'd no doubt offer to show her around, when all she really wanted was to drift along at her own pace. No. She'd done what was necessary, she'd made the call and checked-in. Her time was hers, and hers alone, these last few days.

Euphoria lasted until late afternoon, when Jeanne dug into her handbag for her wallet and found it was missing. The local constable was sympathetic, but there was little he could do besides taking down the report.

'Probably a pickpocket,' he said apologetically. 'We get some of those bad types during the summer, when the tourists are about.'

Jeanne sighed. 'We get them at home, too,' she said. Her eyes searched the man's pleasant face. 'I don't suppose my chances of getting my wallet back are terribly good, are they?'

'I'm afraid not, miss. Did you lose much?'

'Everything but a pocketful of coins,' she said unhappily. 'All my bills, my Visa Card, my traveller's cheques...'

The constable pushed a sheet of paper towards her. 'If you'd be good enough to sign this... Thank you. Well, we'll do what we can. In the meantime, I'd suggest you report the traveller's cheques missing. You can replace them, at least.'

'Yes. But it'll take days.'

The man sighed. 'Is there someone you can contact? Friends? Family?'

She shook her head. 'No,' she said slowly, 'there's no one. I don't know a soul in...'

She paused, and the constable's brows rose. 'Ma'am?'

'Is Warwick the same as Warwickshire?'

He smiled. 'Town and county, as you Americans say.'

'Well, then,' she said with reluctance, 'there is someone.' Sighing, she rummaged in her bag for the slip of paper on which she'd written Graham Caldwell's name and number. 'Yes, here it is. I wonder, Constable, might I use your telephone?'

An hour later, Jeanne was driving along a narrow, twisting road, diligently following the directions given her over the telephone. The woman who'd offered them—Mrs Caldwell—had a pleasant if somewhat quavering voice.

'Abigail Caldwell,' she'd said. 'May I help you?'

Caldwell's wife, Jeanne thought, mentally upping Seth's friend's age from the mid-fifties to mid-seventies.

'Yes,' she said politely. 'I'd like to speak to Graham Caldwell.'

'Mr Caldwell's not in, I'm afraid.'

Disappointed, Jeanne slumped against the wall of the telephone kiosk. 'Do you know when he'll be back?'

'I expect him any time now. May I take a message?'

Well, Jeanne thought, she could always use her last few pence at the tearoom across the street, while she awaited Graham Caldwell's call.

'Yes, please. My name is Jeanne Lester. Mr Caldwell is a friend of my brother Seth's. And——'

It was as far as she got. Mrs Caldwell's voice warmed.

'Oh, my dear, Graham will be so glad you've phoned. He was quite concerned about you.'

Jeanne sighed. Apparently, missing her checkpoint by a few days had been a mistake. By now, Caldwell had no doubt prepared a politely cautioning speech—and heaven only knew what she'd be letting herself in for once he realised she'd managed to lose her wallet. Still, what choice did she have?

'I know he'll want to see you,' Abigail Caldwell said. 'Where are you, dear? In London?'

'No. Actually—actually, I rented a car and drove north. I'm in Warwick.'

'Wonderful! You must join us for dinner. Have you a pencil?'

Jeanne said she had, and, moments later, she'd filled a slip of paper with a series of lefts, rights, and straight-ons. Now, as her car breasted a hill, she wondered if she had got the somewhat confusing directions right.

She had passed a village some miles back. Ahead, as far as the eye could see, lay stone-walled fields. There was no sign of human habitation, except for an imposing old manor house on a grassy hillside.

'We're at Caldwell House,' the old woman had said, 'you'll see the sign.'

And there it was, standing discreetly at the foot of the lane that wound towards a Victorian manor house. Jeanne slowed the car. So much for thatch-roofed cottages, she thought. At least she would eat her humble pie in style.

The door opened at her first knock. A slender, white-haired woman stood in the doorway, leaning lightly on a cane, a questioning smile on her face.

'Miss Lester?'

Jeanne smiled in return. 'Mrs Caldwell?'

'Come in, come in.' The woman moved aside as Jeanne stepped into the house, and the door swung shut. 'How good to see you, dear. Graham's not back yet—I don't know what could be keeping him—but I thought it would be nice if we had a cup of tea while we waited.'

She led the way to a parlour filled with dark furniture and darker family portraits.

'Sit down, please, Miss Lester. How do you take your tea? With milk? Or with lemon?'

'Lemon's fine,' Jeanne said, sinking down on the edge of an overstuffed chesterfield. 'And, please, won't you call me Jeanne?'

'Jeanne it is.' Abigail Caldwell's hand trembled slightly as she handed over a delicate china cup and saucer. 'I just can't wait to see Graham's face when he sees you, dear. He was saying just this morning that he couldn't understand what had happened to you.'

'Nothing,' Jeanne said politely. 'I mean, I meant to phone, but...'

The old woman nodded. 'That's what I told him. "Graham," I said, "I'm quite sure the young lady's been too busy to telephone."' She smiled. 'But you know how fraternity brothers are. When one makes a promise to another, they'll go through Hades to keep it.'

Jeanne managed to smile sweetly. 'And Mr Caldwell promised my brother he'd keep an eye on me while I was in London. How nice of him.'

'Actually, I'm rather glad you looked Graham up here, in Charlecote, instead of in the city.' Mrs Caldwell smiled. 'We wouldn't have had the chance to meet, if you'd phoned Graham in London.'

'Oh, I'm sure we——'

'I hardly ever go to London, you see.'

Jeanne's brows rose. 'You live here, you mean?'

'Yes, of course. I've lived here all my life. More tea, dear?'

Jeanne shook her head. 'No, thank you, Mrs Caldwell. Mr Caldwell commutes, then, to the city?' She smiled politely. 'I thought Americans were the only people crazy enough to drive endless miles to and from their jobs.'

The old woman cocked her head to the side. 'Graham? Oh, he doesn't live here. He has a house in London—a handsome one, on a quiet little street in Mayfair. But he visits me as often as he can.'

A rather sophisticated marriage, Jeanne thought in surprise. But she only nodded, as if the arrangement were commonplace.

'I hope I'm not inconveniencing you, Mrs Caldwell. I wouldn't want to keep you from——'

'Not at all, Jeanne. I love company. In fact, it's one of the nicest things about Graham's visits. I always fill the house with young people when he's here.'

Jeanne's brows shot skyward. 'Do you?'

'Yes.' Abigail leaned forward, and her voice dropped to a whisper. 'He works too hard, I tell him that all the time. And he isn't getting any younger, you know.'

'No,' Jeanne said politely, 'I'm sure he isn't.'

The old woman nodded. 'What he needs,' she said conspiratorially, 'is a wife.'

Jeanne blinked. 'A wife? But——'

A door opened, then slammed. Abigail looked up expectantly, her face wreathed in smiles.

'There he is now,' she said. 'Graham?' Brisk footsteps sounded along the corridor. Jeanne stirred uneasily. For some unknown reason, she felt the hair rise on the nape of her neck. 'Graham, dear, we're in the library.' Abigail's voice rose as the footsteps drew closer. 'Just wait until you see the wonderful surprise I have for you.'

The teacup trembled in Jeanne's hand. She frowned and grasped it more tightly. What was the matter with her? She had lived through two evenings with friends of Seth's. Surely this one would be...

The door swung open and a man stepped inside the room. Tall, broad-shouldered, he was dressed in grey running-shorts and a sleeveless grey T-shirt bearing a faded Harvard logo. There was a bandage on his left hand.

Jeanne stared at him in growing horror. The cup slipped from her suddenly nerveless fingers and clattered against the saucer.

'There you are, Gray,' Abigail said happily. 'And here's Jeanne. Well, aren't you two going to say hello?'

Stunned silence followed the old woman's announcement. Jeanne put down the cup and saucer and rose slowly to her feet, while the room and everything in it swung in a dizzying arc.

The man in the doorway was the same man she had run off the road months before.

He was the man who had tried to lure her to a country inn yesterday afternoon.

He was the man who had been in her bed last night.

Seth's old friend, Graham Caldwell, and the stranger named Gray were one.

Seconds passed, or minutes. Jeanne couldn't be certain of anything except the thundering race of her heart and the incredulous expression on Graham Caldwell's face. He was staring at her as if she were something distasteful he'd tracked into the house on the bottom of his shoes.

It was the way she felt herself.

He was the first to break the silence. 'What are you doing here?' he demanded.

Abigail Caldwell stared at him. 'Graham! What an awful thing to——'

His expression became grim. 'I asked you a question,' he said, striding into the room. Jeanne flinched as he reached out and caught hold of her arm. 'What the hell are you doing here?'

'I—I didn't realise that you——'

'Gray, what on earth is wrong with you?' Abigail leaned heavily on her cane as she rose to her feet. 'This is Jeanne Lester. Your old friend's sister. I thought you'd be delighted to——'

His head swivelled towards his aunt's. 'What did you say?'

'I said, this is Jeanne Lester. Your friend's——'

'Seth's sister?' His face darkened as he turned to Jeanne. 'You're Seth's sweet baby sister?'

A flush rose in her cheeks. 'And you're his old, reliable friend,' she said stiffly. 'How charming.'

Abigail gave a polite little laugh. 'I'm afraid I'm confused,' she said, looking from one of them to the other. 'Have you two met before?'

'Yes,' Jeanne said quickly. 'Your charming nephew...'

She caught her breath as Graham's fingers tightened on her. 'It's a small world, Aunt Abby,' he said. He paused, and then a smile that never quite reached his eyes moved across his mouth. 'Jeanne and I met yesterday, on the road.' He looked down at Jeanne 'She had a flat, and I changed it for her. Isn't that so, Jeanne?'

'I—yes. Yes, that's right. But...'

Abigail's smile was puzzled. 'Is that all? You two seemed—you seemed distressed at the very sight of each other. I thought——'

'We are,' Jeanne said quickly. 'At least, I am. Your nephew——'

'We both are,' Gray said smoothly, slipping his arm around Jeanne's shoulders and holding her so tightly that she knew instinctively her flesh would bear the imprint of his fingers. 'You see, we—we never got around to introducing ourselves.'

The old woman clapped her hands together. 'How charming!' She looked from Gray to Jeanne. 'But you took an immediate liking to each other, of course.'

'No,' Jeanne said quickly, but the sudden pressure of Gray's hand made her gasp.

'Jeanne's too embarrassed to admit it,' he said silkily, 'but yes, you might say that. Isn't that right, Jeanne?'

'You're insane,' she hissed.

'Don't worry about shocking Aunt Abby,' he said. His smile was grim. 'She's quite the romantic. She'll be happy to hear that we made an appointment for dinner.'

'We did no——'

'It's just too bad you backed out at the last minute.' His eyes bored into hers, daring her to contradict him. 'I had hoped to find you waiting for me at the Lygon Arms last evening. But you never showed up.'

Jeanne lifted her chin. He wanted her to lie for him, to pretend that their relationship had been something it had not been. But she wouldn't do it, not even as the risk of whatever his cold, cold eyes promised lay in store for her if she dared defy him.

'What a lovely story,' she said coolly. 'It's just too bad——'

Abigail reached out and clasped her hand. Her touch was dry, almost papery.

'And to think you children didn't even know each other's names.' A smile lit her lined face. 'How lovely. It's just like a book.'

'Mrs Caldwell——'

'Abigail. You must call me Abigail, dear. Oh, I'm just so pleased.' Her fingers squeezed Jeanne's, then fell away, and she began to limp quickly towards the door. 'Let me tell Cook to put out another place for dinner. And I'll have your bags brought in, too. Shall we put her in the rose room, Graham? Or the blue? Which do you think?'

Gray's mouth narrowed. 'I don't think she can stay the night, Aunt Abby.'

'No,' Jeanne said quickly. 'No, I can't.'

'Don't be silly,' the old woman said. 'Certainly she'll stay. The blue room's best, it gets the sun in the morning. And it has its own bath. And...'

The old woman's voice faded, along with her shuffling footsteps. Jeanne and Gray Caldwell stared at each other, and then Jeanne twisted free of his encircling arm.

'You *did* follow me yesterday,' she hissed.

'I did no such thing.'

'No? Then why would you have spent the night at a B and B? You were only a few miles from here!'

Gray smiled coldly. 'I'm sorry to disappoint you, Miss Lester. I stayed the night because I'd got tied up elsewhere. It was late, and I didn't want to wake my aunt.'

Jeanne tossed her head. 'It really doesn't matter,' she said, and she turned and strode towards the door.

'Just where do you think you're going?' His voice curled after her, sharp as the crack of a whip.

'To tell your aunt the truth,' she said, flinging the words at him like stones. 'If you think I'm going to sit at table with you, or sleep beneath your roof——'

He brushed past her and slammed the door shut. 'You'll have to get past me first.'

'Look, you tried that bit last night and I'm not impressed. So if you don't mind...'

Jeanne's words trailed away as he raised his bandaged hand and held it before her.

'See this?' His voice was grim. 'It's a result of your little gift to me last night.' A cold smile tilted across his mouth. 'I've just come from the doctor's office. I've had a tetanus shot, a dose of antibiotics, and the special pleasure of trying to explain how I managed to get a human bite in the first place.' He took a step forward, and Jeanne shrank back. 'I won't need much excuse to even the score, Miss Lester. I promise.'

'Really?' Jeanne said with more courage than she felt. 'And just how will you explain my bruised body to your aunt?'

His eyes narrowed as they raked over her. 'Seth's little sister,' he said softly. 'Seth's sweet, innocent baby sister.'

'Look,' she said through her teeth, 'I don't know what my brother told you about me, but——'

'Nothing that was true, obviously.' His voice was hard and cold. 'The poor bastard feels guilty about having tried to railroad you into marriage.'

'Mr Caldwell, this is hardly the time to——'

'I wonder what he'd say if he knew you ran away from your wedding so you could meet another man?'

Jeanne stared at him. 'What are you talking about? I didn't...'

He waved his hand dismissively. 'I never dreamed that was you on the road that night. It was just bad luck that dragged me into that mess: I was in the area on business, and I phoned Seth just to say hello. "Come on over," he said, "have a drink—my little sister's getting married." '

'Look, you don't know anything about that. I was——'

'I know that the guy you met on the road was the one you'd been living with in New York, the one you'd run out on so you could marry some poor S.O.B. you thought you could lead around by the nose.'

She flushed. 'You're wrong. Dead wrong.'

'Seth told me everything that night. We had a couple of stiff drinks while we waited for you to come back.'

Gray smiled unpleasantly. 'You didn't, of course. You and your lover were too busy.'

'Damn you, that's not——'

'What went wrong, little sister?' His lips drew back from his teeth. 'Did you change your mind again?'

Jeanne's mouth opened, then snapped shut. 'I don't owe you any explanations,' she muttered. 'Now, if you'll just step aside...'

His hands clamped tightly on her shoulders. 'And then there's the way you came on to me. Hell, poor Seth. If he had any idea——'

Her head came up sharply. 'Came on to you? Me?' Jeanne gave a short, bitter laugh. 'That's a good one, Mr Caldwell. Really slick. *You* were the one who tried to talk me into sleeping with him ten minutes after we met. *You* were the one who forced himself into my bed last night. *You* were the one who damned near raped me.'

A sly smile curved across his mouth. 'Rape? It's not called rape when the lady is ready and willing. And you certainly were that.' His hands slid up her shoulders, along her neck to her jaw. 'I'm still wondering why I didn't take what you so generously offered.'

Jeanne's face flamed. 'That's a lie.'

His smile twisted, grew knowing and dark. 'You were on fire in my arms, little sister.' He moved closer to her; she could see the sudden beat of a pulse in his jaw. 'Warm. Willing. Eager.'

'I—I threw you out,' she whispered.

'Yeah.' His smile faded, and his gaze moved slowly over her face, lingering on her mouth. 'And I've been wondering about that, too.' She caught her breath as he tilted her face to his. 'Maybe that was all part of the act. Maybe I was right about you—that you'd planted yourself in my bed.' Jeanne began to struggle frantically against him. He pushed against her, and she was propelled back against the wall, the hard, hot weight of his body pressing against hers. 'Maybe what you wanted was just a little encouragement.'

'No. No, you're wrong.'

His breath warmed her face. 'I think you wanted to be taken,' he whispered. He bent towards her as he held her face imprisoned in his hands. 'And I think I should have accommodated.'

She closed her eyes as his mouth touched hers. 'Don't,' she said. 'Damn you, don't.'

Her angry plea was lost in his kiss. His lips were cool, hard against hers, and she struggled to twist her face away. But he was too strong for her and, after a few seconds, a slow, insidious heat began moving slowly through her veins.

She whimpered softly as his kiss eased, changed from something given in anger to something else—and then, with a suddenness that left her gasping, his hands fell away from her and he stepped back.

Their eyes met, and his lips drew back from his teeth again. 'Seth doesn't know you at all, does he, Miss Lester?'

Jeanne stared at him. Her heart was thudding so loudly she was certain he could hear it.

She took a deep breath. 'Get out of my way, please,' she said calmly.

He folded his arms across his chest and shook his head. 'You're not going anywhere.'

'Look, you've had your fun. Now, step aside before I——'

'My aunt is an old woman, Miss Lester. She lives on enough medications to keep a pharmacy in business. If you think I'm going to let you say anything to upset her——'

'Your aunt's health isn't my problem,' Jeanne said through her teeth. She stared back at him, meeting his angry glare with one of her own, and then she slumped back against the wall. 'All right, I won't tell her the truth. I'll let you off easy, for her sake.'

He looked down at her, as if he were measuring her with his eyes, and then he nodded.

'Good. Believe me, the prospect of spending an evening in your company doesn't please me any more than it does you. But we're both adults; we can manage. And then, in the morning——'

'I didn't say I'd go through with this charade,' Jeanne said quickly. 'I simply said——'

There was a discreet knock at the door. They looked towards it as it swung open.

'Cook says she'll make that sherry trifle you like for dessert, Graham,' Abigail said. 'Nancy's brought your suitcase in, Jeanne. I told her to unpack for you. She'll press whatever might need doing.'

Jeanne shook her head. 'Oh, but—but . . .'

The old woman smiled and held out her hand. 'Let me show you to your room. I'm sure you want to freshen up before dinner. Graham, you've just time to change before drinks. I think we'll have wine with dinner this evening. Perhaps a bottle of that nice Sauvignon. Would you bring one up from the cellar?'

Jeanne glanced back helplessly as the old woman led her towards the stairs. Graham Caldwell glared at her, his expression of cold resignation, she was certain, a duplicate of her own.

She was trapped, at least until tomorrow morning. There was no choice but to make the best of fate's incredibly bizarre joke.

CHAPTER FIVE

UNDER other circumstances, Jeanne would have been
delighted with the room to which Abigail Caldwell led
her. Unlike the downstairs parlour, the blue bedroom
was large and airy. Sunlight streamed in through frothy
white curtains and dappled the old-fashioned four-poster
bed with gold. Charming floral prints hung on the walls,
and there was a delicate scent of lavender in the air.

But it was difficult to pay the handsome room the
compliments it deserved. Jeanne tried hard, for Mrs
Caldwell's sake, saying what she hoped were the right
things about the French armoire in the corner and the
old glass perfume bottles that lined the dressing-table.
She smiled politely as the old woman rambled on happily
about the room's history—it had hosted the young
Victoria, Abigail said proudly, and, in more recent years,
an actress whose name Jeanne recognised from the days
of black and white films.

But her thoughts were concentrated on Graham
Caldwell. She could still see the dark expression on his
face as his aunt had led her from the library. All the
way up the wide, curving staircase, she'd been sure she
could feel his eyes boring into her back.

She'd had to fight back the desire to spin around and
tell him that whatever he felt for her was mutual. And
now, here she was, not only forced to be a guest in this
house but forced to pretend she was happy about it.

It was an impossible situation. But it wasn't Abigail
Caldwell's fault. And, even without Gray beside her to
keep her from telling the old woman the truth, Jeanne
couldn't be that unkind.

His aunt was too warm and hospitable.

67

One evening, she thought as Abigail prattled on, just one evening. I can certainly manage that.

After a few moments, Abigail laughed self-consciously. 'Forgive me,' she said. 'I tend to go on.' Jeanne began to protest, but the old woman shook her head. 'I suppose it's just that it's such a pleasure to have a friend of Graham's come to visit, dear.' She leaned forward, her eyes searching for a hidden eavesdropper, her voice a whisper. 'He's never brought anyone here before, you know.'

He hadn't quite brought her, either, Jeanne thought, but she only nodded.

Abigail's lips drew up in a smile as she smoothed imaginary wrinkles from the blue and white bedspread.

'And he's invited you to stay the night. I can't tell you how pleased that makes me.'

Jeanne looked at her helplessly. That wasn't exactly what had happened. But she didn't have the heart to correct her elderly hostess. Besides, what did it matter? One evening. She only had to manage one evening...

'It warms my heart to see the way he looks at you, dear.' Abigail put her hand lightly on Jeanne's, her touch light as an autumn leaf. 'Such intensity, if you know what I mean.'

Jeanne swallowed. 'Yes,' she said. 'Such intensity.' She hesitated. She didn't want to hurt Gray's aunt. But the woman was putting a delicate twist on things. And then there was the way Gray had shaded the story of their meeting—all in all, their non-existent relationship was developing a life and substance of its own.

'Mrs Caldwell...'

'Abigail. Please, do call me Abigail.'

Jeanne moistened her lips with the tip of her tongue. 'Abigail,' she said gently, 'I—I wouldn't want you to get the wrong idea about—about your nephew and me. We—er—we've only just met, you see, and...'

Abigail smiled. 'Believe me, dear, I know the world's not the same as it was when I was a girl.' Her lips twitched. 'Caldwell House and I may both look like relics, but our hearts are very much up to date. I think it's lovely that you and Gray met in such a charming way.' One pale blue eye closed in a delicate wink. 'What's the point of formalities, I always say, if all they do is keep people apart? Isn't that right?'

It wasn't, Jeanne knew. At least, it wasn't, not the way Abigail Caldwell meant it.

But she could only nod her head and smile weakly. 'Yes,' she said. 'I suppose so.'

The old woman smiled, too. 'Now, then, drinks in the parlour at seven.' She stepped into the hall. 'Dinner at seven-thirty. If you need anything in the meantime, just ring for Nancy.'

The door swung gently shut. Jeanne stared at it, then sank down on the edge of the bed.

What she needed was a way out of this nightmare. But there was none, not until morning.

Sighing, she began stripping off her clothing. She'd glimpsed an assortment of bath oils and lotions in the en suite bathroom. A long, hot soak might relax her.

Something had to, or she doubted if she'd get through drinks and dinner without marching up to Graham Caldwell and slinging a glass of wine in his handsome face.

It was, she thought grimly, going to be a very long evening.

At ten minutes past seven, Jeanne came slowly down the carpeted stairs, straining to hear the sound of voices from the floor below. Abigail had sounded as if she expected her guest to be prompt, but Jeanne was unwilling to find herself in the drawing-room alone with Gray if she could possibly avoid it. She had waited in her room while the hands of a delicate French clock moved slowly past the hour, and then, finally, she'd sighed, risen to her feet, and walked to the old-fashioned cheval mirror standing in the corner.

She had dressed for dinner, or, at least, as close to it as she'd ever come. At Kristin's urging, she'd packed two long gowns in her suitcase.

'There's no point in taking them,' she'd insisted.

But her sister-in-law had been gently persuasive. 'They don't take up any room at all,' Kristin had said, folding the wispy bits of silk and lace and tucking them away. 'And who knows? You might just meet some handsome guy and want to knock his eyes out.'

Jeanne had smiled and given in. Now, she was glad she had—but not for the reasons Kristin had suggested.

Looking at herself in the mirror, she'd smoothed down the skirt of the gown she was wearing, a breast- and hip-skimming fall of soft black silk with long sleeves and a deep V neckline.

If she'd assessed things correctly, people in this house dressed for dinner. Well, she'd thought, lifting her chin at her reflection, as long as she was here, she'd play her role properly.

She knew Graham Caldwell thought she was something less than a lady. She was determined to prove him wrong. Living well was the best revenge, wasn't that what they said?

Perhaps behaving well would prove even more satisfying.

Now, as she reached the foot of the steps, Jeanne paused. The moment's courage she'd gained seeing herself in the mirror was fast fading. She might look like a sophisticate but just now she felt like a child at a masquerade party.

Her heart skipped a beat and thudded against her ribs. This was ridiculous! She was letting Graham Caldwell intimidate her, and for what? He was the one who'd behaved badly, not she, just as he was the one who'd insisted on this foolish charade.

Jeanne squared her shoulders. She would be every inch the lady tonight. Let the bastard make what he could out of that.

She paused at the parlour door. She could hear voices within, Abigail's light, fluting soprano a counterpoint to her nephew's deep baritone. There was a sudden fluttering in the pit of her stomach but she ignored it. Quickly, she took one last, deep inhalation, then stepped into the room.

The room seemed brighter now, with lights lit and the french doors open to the evening air. Gray and his aunt were at the far end, their backs to her.

Jeanne wiped her palms on her skirt, then forced a smile to her face.

'Good evening,' she said. They turned towards her, and her smile trembled a little. Gray was wearing a dark dinner suit, his hair was still damp—from the shower, she thought—and he looked handsome enough to take Jeanne's breath away.

Abigail smiled. 'Come in, dear. How lovely you look. Doesn't she look lovely, Graham?'

Gray took a step forward. His eyes moved over her slowly, lingering on the soft curve of her breasts, travelling down the length of her body, then returning to her face. The look in his eyes was bored, almost dismissive.

'You're late,' he said shortly. 'We've been waiting for you.'

Jeanne flushed. 'Sorry. I—I took a bath and I guess I lost track of the time.'

'Wine?' A cool smile curved over his mouth as he held a glass of dark red liquid out to her. 'You *are* old enough to drink, aren't you, Jeannie?'

She felt her flush deepen. 'It's Jeanne,' she said, pleased with how calm she sounded. 'And yes, thank you, I'm old enough.'

The cool smile came again. 'Yes. I'm certain you are.'

She took the glass from him. Their fingers brushed, and the heat of his touch seemed to race along her skin.

'Thank you.'

He nodded, then turned his back to her. 'As I was saying, Aunt Abby, that roof needs fixing. And the chimney, as well. I'll make arrangements to have them taken care of while I'm here, so you won't have to be bothered with workmen coming and going once I've returned to London.'

Abigail nodded. 'Whatever you think, Graham.' She looked past him to Jeanne and smiled. 'Gray takes such good care of me,' she said. 'No man could be kinder.'

No man could be colder, was more like it, Jeanne thought, as she smiled politely in return. Gray had paid her no more attention than he would a servant, and the way he'd looked at her had told her very clearly what he thought of the way she was dressed.

She had worn this gown once before, the night she and George had set the date for their wedding, and George had not been able to keep his eyes off her. In fact, she'd thought later that wearing it had probably marked the beginning of the end. George had wanted to make love to her that night, and she'd wanted to let him—but when he'd started to inch the gown from her shoulder, a tremor had gone through her, not of pleasure but of distaste, and she'd known then, deep in her heart, that something was terribly wrong between them.

Gray hadn't even noticed the way the silk clung to her body, or the delicate rise of her breasts within the low neckline. Correction, she thought. He had noticed, but he hadn't given a damn.

Not that she wanted him to, of course. She had worn the gown because it was formal and proper, not to catch his eye. But he might at least...

'...you fly home?'

Jeanne's gaze flew to Abigail's. The old woman was smiling at her, clearly waiting for her to answer whatever question it was that she'd asked.

Jeanne swallowed drily. 'I'm sorry, Abigail. Did you...?'

'Abigail?' Gray's dark brows rose as he turned to her, and a sardonic smile flitted across his mouth. 'How cosy.'

'It was your aunt's suggestion that I call her that,' Jeanne said. 'If you don't approve——'

The old woman stepped between them. 'Dinner must be ready by now,' she said, looping her arm through Jeanne's. 'Gray? Bring the wine along with us, won't you? We don't want to let such a fine old bottle go to waste.'

The dining-room was lit by elaborate candelabra, the table set with Spode china, Waterford crystal, and fine old sterling cutlery. The food was equally gracious.

But the meal seemed interminable. Jeanne was painfully aware of Gray's determination to ignore her. Not that he was impolite: he was far too clever for that. It was just that he never initiated any conversation between them. It was always his aunt who did so, and then he who had no choice but to follow through.

Jeanne's discomfort grew. Having her here was his idea, not hers. And his treatment of her was unfair. She wasn't a pariah, although he was treating her as one.

'More wine, Jeanne?'

Gray's voice was smooth. She looked across the table at him, her cheeks flushing when she saw the mockery in his eyes.

She had had enough to drink. More than enough: she was having trouble eating. Still, what did it matter? The wine, at least, went down smoothly.

'Yes,' she said recklessly. 'Thank you.'

'Jeanne?' Abigail smiled at her. 'You never did answer my question, dear. When are you flying home?'

'Jeanne's leaving the day after tomorrow.' Gray's mouth curved in the hint of a smile. 'Isn't that right, Jeanne?'

Their eyes met. 'Yes,' she said. 'That's right.'

Abigail sighed. 'That's unfortunate. I'd hoped you would be staying on for a bit. I'd planned on asking you to spend the rest of your holiday here, at Caldwell House.'

The look on Gray's face brought a macabre pleasure to Jeanne's heart.

'And I'd have accepted,' she said pleasantly. 'If only I were staying.'

His aunt smiled delightedly. 'Well, then, at least you'll stay on tomorrow.'

Jeanne stared at her. 'No,' she said quickly. 'I mean, I'd be happy to. But—but I have to get back to London. My rental car...'

'Nonsense. Gray will see to it that your car is returned, won't you, dear?'

A muscle tightened in his jaw. 'If Jeanne has to get back, Abigail, we can't very well stop her.'

'And we'll get you back to the city in plenty of time for you to catch your flight the next day,' Abigail said, as if no one had offered any objections.

'Aunt Abby——'

His aunt put her index finger to her mouth. 'I'll just phone Kerry Osborne in the morning and tell her we'll have to cancel tomorrow night's dinner.'

Gray's brows rose. 'Kerry Osborne?'

'Yes. You remember Kerry, don't you? That pretty, red-haired girl, the one you met at the Christmas party last year?'

He sighed and leaned back in his chair. 'I don't know,' he said wryly. 'You managed to fill the house with pretty girls that day, as usual.'

Abigail's laughter was good-humoured. 'Well, Kerry remembers you, dear. She's looking forward to seeing you tomorrow night. But I'll postpone our dinner until Tuesday. And I'll move Sally Dietrich over to Friday.'

'Don't do that on my account,' Jeanne said quickly. 'I can't stay, anyway.' She glanced at Gray and gave him the first genuine smile of the evening. 'What your nephew said was quite accurate—I have to get back to London.'

Gray's eyes narrowed. 'Now that I think about it,' he said softly, 'I think Abby's right.'

Jeanne stared at him. 'You do?'

He gave her the same slow, sexy smile that had set her heart racing the first time they'd met.

'Absolutely. I'll arrange for someone from the village to return your car.'

'Oh, but I wouldn't want to put you to any trouble——'

He leaned towards her and put his hand over hers where it lay on the table.

'And I'll drive you to London first thing in the morning the next day. How's that sound?'

'It sounds—it sounds...'

She wanted to tell him it sounded impossible. But he was looking at her so strangely, as if it were last night all over again, as if...

A flush of heat rose within her. The wine, she thought, as the room tilted, I've had too much wine.

Abigail pushed her chair back from the table. 'Good,' she said briskly, 'that's all settled, then. I'll tell Kerry we'll expect her on Sunday evening.' Her brow furrowed. 'Or did I ask the Darby sisters over for that night?'

Gray's hand slipped from Jeanne's. 'Abigail,' he said warningly, and his aunt rose quickly to her feet.

'Never mind. I'll check my appointment book in the morning.' She waved her hand as her nephew stood up. 'No, no, stay where you are, Graham. I'm going to the kitchen to check on our trifle.' Her cane tapped lightly across the polished oak floor. 'Where is that girl when you want her? Nancy? Nancy!' She paused at the door and glanced back. 'Graham, why don't you show Jeanne the garden? I'll just be a few minutes.'

Silence fell across the room, and then Gray sighed.

'I suppose I'd better show it to you,' he said with dry irony. 'She'll probably do a quiz on the flower-beds when she gets back.'

It was impossible not to smile. 'All right.' Jeanne tossed her napkin on her plate and got to her feet. 'Actually, I could use some fresh air. It's awfully warm in here, isn't it?'

A smile twitched at the corners of his mouth. 'Do you think so?'

She nodded. 'Mmm. I feel almost light-headed.'

Gray took her arm as they stepped out of the french doors into the night.

'I just want to make sure you don't trip over anything,' he said when she tried to pull free. 'We wouldn't want to send damaged goods home to Seth, would we?'

Jeanne looked up at him quickly, but his face was impossible to see in the darkness of the garden.

'I'm fine,' she said stiffly. 'I just had a little too much wine.'

His hand tightened on her. '*Omni excedere*. Everything to excess, is that the way you do it?'

'Listen here, Mr Caldwell——'

'Careful,' he said coolly. 'There's a loose piece of slate just ahead.'

'I assure you, I'm perfectly capable of taking care of myself.'

'Oh, I'm ready to believe that,' he said, his voice silken. 'But it might come as a hell of a shock to Seth to find out that his sweet little sister isn't...'

Jeanne pulled free of his hand and spun towards him. 'Isn't what?' she demanded. 'Come on, Mr Caldwell, you might as well spit it out. I know what you think of me.'

The moon, caught in the low branches of a flowering plum tree, painted his face with pale shadow.

'What I think,' he said coldly, 'is that you've done one hell of a job deceiving everybody.'

'Not as good a job as you've done,' Jeanne said with equal coldness. 'Your aunt has you pegged as the soul of chivalry.' Her husky voice became a purr. 'I wonder what she'd think if she knew you were in the habit of climbing into the beds of strange women and trying to rape them?'

Gray's jaw thrust forward. 'Are we back to that?' A tight smile curled over his mouth. 'I guess I've been away from the States longer than I thought, if the way you greeted me is the definition of rape.'

Jeanne drew a deep breath. 'You know what I mean. You forced yourself on me. And if your aunt knew——'

'She wouldn't believe it, because it's a lie.' His voice was flat. 'And we both know it.'

She felt the swift rise of heat in her cheeks. 'It's not a lie. I—I...' Jeanne fell silent. After a moment, she cleared her throat. 'Look,' she said quickly, 'what happened last night was—it was a mistake. I—I don't really know how to explain it.'

Gray puffed out his breath. 'Don't you?'

'No. No matter what you think——'

'What I think,' he said harshly, 'is that we're both adults.' He drew to a halt and clasped her shoulders, turning her to him. 'That *is* what you are, isn't it? Despite your brother's rose-coloured belief in the sanctity of his little sister.'

Jeanne's throat felt dry as sandpaper. 'Yes,' she whispered. 'I mean, I'm an adult, of course. But——'

His hands tightened on her. 'Well, then. Adults have needs. They don't have to apologise for admitting that they want to go to bed together.'

She felt her face flame, and she was grateful for the protection of the shadowy darkness.

'It wasn't like that, Mr Caldwell.'

'Gray,' he said softly. His hands slid to her face and tilted it to his. 'I thought we'd settled that already.'

Jeanne drew in her breath. 'Please. You really don't understand.'

She fell silent. What could she say to him? She looked up, trying to read his face in the pale moonlight. Maybe what he'd just said, as brutal as it sounded, was the truth.

Adults have needs. Those had been his very words, and how could she deny it? She had wanted his kisses last night, she had wanted to lose herself in his arms.

But that didn't make sense. Why would she be overcome by desire for a stranger, when she had never felt that way before? Not with Charlie, even after they'd shared a flat for weeks. Not with George, even after his ring was on her finger.

The abandon she'd felt with Graham Caldwell was stunningly new. But she couldn't tell him that. It was too embarrassing; it only made the way she'd behaved last night even harder to understand.

Anyway, he would never believe her. He'd only think she was lying, just as he thought she'd been lying to Seth all this time.

His hands threaded into her hair. 'Well?' he asked softly. 'What is it I don't understand?'

Jeanne let out her breath. What did it matter what his opinion of her was? After tomorrow, they would never see each other again.

'That you frightened me,' she said. 'Finding you in my bed—the whole thing was terrifying.' She met his gaze. 'I think you owe me an apology.'

He looked at her for a long moment, and then he smiled. 'And I think you might be right,' he said, his voice soft as he lowered his head towards her. 'What happened last night was artless. The only defence I can offer is that you took me by surprise.' He smiled again, this time so intimately that Jeanne's pulse quickened. 'Finding you in my bed, all warm and soft with sleep— I'm afraid I got carried away.'

'Gray——'

'Believe me, Jeanne, I know you deserve better.' His mouth brushed lightly over hers. 'Moonlight,' he said. 'And the scent of flowers.'

'Don't,' she said, but even as the whispered plea left her lips, her head dropped back. A tremor raced through her as his mouth pressed against the curving juncture of neck and shoulder.

The silk fabric of her gown sighed against her skin as Gray's lips nuzzled it off her shoulder. His teeth closed lightly in the bared flesh, and Jeanne moaned softly. Her hands came up between them and lay lightly against him.

Gray lifted his head and looked at her. 'There should have been flowers, Jeanne. And candlelight.'

Like tonight, she thought suddenly, and all at once reality returned.

Last night had been artless, he'd said, and now he was going to make up for it.

She was being seduced. And by a master.

The realisation brought a strange chill to her heart. She pushed her hands against his chest.

'Stop,' she said sharply. She drew a deep breath. 'I think—I think we should go inside.' Her voice was cool; in some distant part of her mind she thought with surprise that she barely recognised it as her own. 'Your aunt will be looking for us.'

There was a silence. She felt the surge of Gray's heart beneath her fingertips, then the whisper of his touch along her cheek, the heat of his palm against her throat, the brush of his fingers on the soft swell of her breasts as they rose above her gown.

For a moment, the world stood still. Then, without warning, his hands fell away.

'Yes,' he said in a voice that matched the impersonal coolness of hers, 'you're quite right. I'm sure she will.'

Gray took her hand, tucked it into his arm, and together they walked back to the lighted safety of the house.

CHAPTER SIX

CALDWELL HOUSE lay silent in the early morning. Jeanne's bedroom, so cheerful and pleasant yesterday afternoon, was dark and sombre in the grey light.

It was going to rain, she thought, as she punched up the pillows and sat up in bed. The skies were an uncompromising pewter, and there was a smell of dampness in the air.

She groaned softly as she moved her head. There was a faint tattoo in her temple. Too much wine and not enough sleep, that's what had done it. And it was Gray's fault.

If only she hadn't drunk so much at dinner.

If only he hadn't kissed her in the garden.

If only she hadn't kissed him back.

If only...

Jeanne muttered an unladylike word and swung the blankets aside. What was done, was done, her mother always said, and it was true.

But you didn't have to repeat your mistakes, either. Gray Caldwell had taken advantage of her twice, but he wouldn't get the chance to do it again.

Anyway, she thought, snatching up her brush and pulling it through her hair, she'd probably hardly see the man today.

'I've appointments with contractors all day long,' he'd said to his aunt last night when she'd suggested, over coffee, that he might want to show Jeanne the surrounding countryside.

His voice had been cold, almost contemptuous. Jeanne had flushed. She was sure she knew why he was angry: she had rejected his advances in the garden, just as she had rejected him the night before.

But his aunt hadn't seemed to notice. 'That's all right,' she'd said pleasantly. 'I'll just take Jeanne along with me to the village, shall I, dear?' Abigail had said briskly, and Jeanne had nodded.

'Yes,' she'd said, 'that sounds like fun.'

The truth was that she'd have probably said the same thing about a trip to the dentist. Anything would have sounded better than spending the day in Gray's company.

After that, he'd said nothing more. Abigail had settled Jeanne on the couch beside her, and Gray took a seat in a far corner of the room and opened the evening paper.

'Now,' his aunt had said briskly, 'let's get to know each other.'

Somehow, Jeanne had managed to keep up her end of a polite conversation. But, although she couldn't see Gray's face clearly, she'd been aware that he wasn't reading at all. His eyes had never left her.

Gradually, Jeanne had become conscious of how she must look. Her hand stole up to her tousled hair, to her flushed cheeks, and finally she tugged lightly at the neckline of her dress to ensure that she'd pulled it back on to her shoulder. The skin his teeth had grazed lay hidden, but it had tingled beneath the silk. Her eyes had swept across the room to Gray, and suddenly he'd risen and stood beside his chair.

'I've a long day ahead of me tomorrow,' he'd said. 'If you'll both excuse me?'

Abigail had offered her cheek for his kiss, and Jeanne had nodded her goodnight rather than trust her voice. Not long after, the old woman had yawned delicately, and she and Jeanne had gone up to their rooms.

She had been tired. But she hadn't slept very well, Jeanne thought now as she slipped off her nightgown. She had drifted in and out of dark, formless dreams, wishing she'd packed a book or a magazine in her things, until finally the clock read seven a.m.

It was early, but it was a respectable time to start the day. Once she was dressed, she'd tiptoe downstairs and...

Her breath caught as she glimpsed herself in the mirror. There was a faint bruise on her shoulder, the imprint left by Gray's teeth. Jeanne's hand lifted to it. Her skin felt warm; her eyes closed slowly as she remembered the feel of his mouth, the heat of his breath...

'Enough!'

Quickly, she stalked across the room, yanked open the armoire, and pulled on shorts, T-shirt, and running-shoes.

What she needed was fresh air. A jog along the narrow lane that led to the main road would do just fine. By the time the rest of the house was stirring, she'd be showered and dressed for the day.

The stairs creaked lightly beneath her feet as she made her way down them. The smell of coffee warned her that she wasn't the first person up, but she'd assumed that the cook or housekeeper would already be busy in the kitchen.

But the kitchen was empty. Jeanne poured herself some coffee from the American-style coffee-maker on the counter, then started down the hall towards the rear of the house. Surely there was a back door; it might be quieter to go out that way.

Halfway down the hall, she paused. There was a sound coming from behind the closed door to her right, a rhythmic thudding that sounded as if someone was bouncing a ball against the floor. Curious, Jeanne hesitated, then stepped closer to it.

The door opened at a touch. A large room stretched before her. It seemed barren at first, and then she realised that it wasn't a room at all. It was a gymnasium. Exercise mats lay in one corner; an exercise bicycle stood nearby. There was a complicated-looking, squat machine opposite—and there was Gray, his back to her, working out on the far side of the room.

Jeanne's breath caught. The sound she'd heard was the sound of his feet slapping against a rubber mat as he skipped. He was wearing shorts as disreputable as the ones she'd seen him in yesterday, and a sweatshirt with the sleeves cut out.

Boxers skipped—she knew that. But somehow she'd always thought of it as a girl's game.

Until now.

Sweat darkened Gray's shirt and gleamed like diamonds in his dark hair. His muscles knotted as they moved beneath his skin. There was nothing even remotely feminine about him, she thought, as she watched him. He looked powerful and very masculine.

The windows were open to catch the morning breeze, and his scent came to her on the air, clean and sharp and laced with sweat and leather.

Jeanne took a step back. She didn't belong here, watching him like this. And she didn't want to see him. Not just yet. Not when she was dressed this way, not when he was...

Gray tossed the rope aside and stretched his arms towards the ceiling. Tugging his sweatshirt over his head, he strolled towards the rear of the gym while he towelled his body dry with the crumpled shirt.

Say something, Jeanne told herself fiercely. Say something, before he...

His hands slipped into the elastic waistband of his shorts and he began tugging them down.

'Good morning.'

Her voice was quick, almost breathless. He hesitated, then turned towards her while he pulled the shorts back into place.

'Good morning.' His tone was even, his face expressionless.

Jeanne swallowed drily. 'I didn't mean to intrude,' she said. 'I mean, I—I heard a noise and...'

Gray stared at her in silence, and then, to her relief, he smiled.

'That's all right,' he said. She watched as he pulled a clean sweatshirt from where it lay draped across a chinning bar and tugged it down over his head. 'I didn't think you'd be up this early.'

She smiled hesitantly. 'I've always been an early riser. Besides, I didn't sleep very...'

Her voice tapered off as their eyes met. 'No,' he said drily. 'I didn't, either.' His glance fell to the mug she held, forgotten, in her hand. 'Have you had breakfast yet?'

Jeanne stared at him blankly. 'Have I...?' She looked down at her half-finished coffee. 'Oh. No. No, I haven't. I just—I smelled the coffee, so I helped myself. I hope that was all right.'

Gray smiled. 'Sure, assuming you can stand drinking the stuff.' He walked slowly towards her. 'I made it myself.'

'Did you? Well, it's good. Very good.' She fell silent. This was silly. Why did she feel as if she were back in high school, standing in a corridor and talking to a boy who'd left her tongue-tied? She took a deep breath. 'Well, I'll let you get back to—to whatever it is you were doing.'

'What I'm doing,' he said, tossing the sweatshirt aside, 'is working off that meal Abigail fed us last night.' He grinned. 'Especially the trifle.'

Jeanne had to smile. 'I know what you mean. What was in it, anyway? Custard, raspberries...'

'A thousand calories, that's what was in it.' Gray ran his hands through his hair, pushing the damp strands back from his forehead. 'The old girl kills me with kindness, whenever I visit. That's why I had this room converted.'

'Ah. I see. A place of penance.'

He laughed. 'Something like that.'

They fell silent. After a moment, Jeanne cleared her throat.

'I'll be going now,' she said.

Gray's hand fell lightly on her shoulder as she started to turn away.

'That's a great outfit,' he said. She glanced back at him, and he gave her a lazy smile. She flushed lightly as his eyes moved over her. 'Do you wear it because it looks good, or do you run?'

Jeanne ran her tongue along her lips. 'I run. Well, not run. I jog. A little, anyway.'

'Good. I can use the company.'

Her head came up. 'What?'

'I run every morning, when I'm at home.' He knelt and retied the laces of his running-shoes. 'You're welcome to join me, if you like.'

She looked at him in amazement as he straightened up and smiled at her. Was this the same Graham Caldwell who'd treated her so coldly yesterday, who'd barely spoken a civilised word to her after she'd rejected him again last night?

It was as if he'd read her mind. His smile tilted a little, and he put his hands on his hips.

'Do you remember what you said last night? That I owed you an apology? Well, you were right.'

'Gray, I don't think we should——'

'You and I got off to a bad start,' he said. 'And it doesn't make any sense, when you come right down to it.'

Jeanne stared up at him. 'What do you mean?'

He sighed and raked his fingers through his dark hair again. 'What I mean, Jeannie, is that your brother is one of my oldest friends. We bummed around Europe together, the summer he graduated from Harvard. Did he tell you?'

'No. I mean, yes, he mentioned Europe. But——'

'Seth, another guy who'd just got his degree, and me.' He grinned. 'They never let me forget that I was there on sufferance. Me, just entering my second year, with two older men.'

Jeanne smiled, too. 'Yes. I can imagine.'

'The thing is, I'd like us to be friends.'

Her eyes widened. 'You would?'

'Yes. Just because we met under less than ideal circumstances...'

She felt her cheeks grow warm. 'About that...'

'Hey, you don't owe me any explanations. I'll admit, I was a little confused—I mean, Seth had me on the look-out for his baby sister, not someone like...' He hesitated, and for a second Jeanne thought she saw something dark and calculating glitter in his eyes. But then he smiled again, and she knew she must have been wrong.

'I didn't expect you to be so grown up,' he said. 'It came as a shock.'

She sighed. 'Well,' she said slowly, 'I suppose...'

Gray put out his hand. 'Friends?'

Jeanne looked at him. 'Friends,' she said, putting her hand in his.

They stood that way for a moment, smiling into each other's eyes, and then Gray let go of her.

'OK, little sister. Let's see if you can stay with me.'

An hour later, Jeanne was more than ready to admit she couldn't. They had jogged down the lane to the road, to the crossroads, and then they'd started back. By the time they reached the house, sweat was pouring off her and she was gasping for air. She groaned when Gray trotted past the house and into the field beyond. When she finally reached the copse of trees and the old stone wall where he was waiting, she could hardly breathe.

'OK?' he asked.

Jeanne nodded. 'OK,' she wheezed, collapsing back against the wall beside him. A light breeze blew across the meadow, and she shivered under its touch.

'Here,' Gray said, putting his arm around her and drawing her against him, 'let me warm you.'

'I'm fine,' she gasped. 'Really.'

'Just lean into me,' he said, ignoring her protests. 'Take deep breaths. Good.' He glanced down at her and smiled. 'You did all right, little sister. I didn't think you'd keep up, but you did.'

Little sister. Why did the teasing nickname grate so?

Jeanne smiled back at him. 'We aim to please,' she said lightly.

He gave her a quick grin. 'Tell me, does Seth know what a great runner you are?'

She shrugged her shoulders and stepped away from him. 'I'm not "great". I just——'

'I'll bet he doesn't know very much about you at all.'

Jeanne's head tilted as she looked up at him. He was still smiling, but there was a hardness about his mouth.

'What's that supposed to mean?' she asked carefully.

His eyes darkened, but his smile stayed fixed. 'Just what I said. Your brother's got this view of you that isn't quite realistic. Isn't that right?'

She leaned back against the wall, watching him. 'You might say that, I guess.'

'You guess.' There *was* something wrong with his smile, she could see it clearly now. It looked almost wolfish, as if he were having trouble keeping it from becoming a snarl. Jeanne shivered again. 'I wonder—couldn't we have this conversation over breakfast?' She took a step forward. 'I've worked up an appetite. And——'

Gray's hand clamped tightly over her shoulder. 'I'd rather we talked here,' he said. 'Away from Abigail.'

'Away from...?'

'Yes.' He drew in his breath, then expelled it. 'She likes you,' he said. His hand fell away from her. 'I suppose you know that.'

A puzzled smile moved across Jeanne's face. 'Well, I like her, too. She's a charming lady.'

'Umm. If she has one fault, it's that she finds it difficult to let me lead my own life.'

How familiar that sounded. Jeanne sighed. 'That can be rough.'

He nodded. 'Yes, it can.'

She laughed softly. 'She's an inveterate matchmaker, isn't she? All that talk about dinners and teas...'

He grinned as he leaned back against the wall and crossed his arms over his chest. 'Exactly. She feels that I haven't shown any interest in carrying on the Caldwell name, you see.'

Jeanne brushed her wind-blown hair back from her face. 'I can't believe there aren't women in your life,' she said lightly.

'Women? Yes, of course. What Abigail wants is one woman, a special one.'

'And there's no one like that,' she said, watching his face.

He shook his head. 'No. Absolutely not. I've no intention of marrying. Not for a long, long time, anyway.'

A little knot seemed to lodge in her throat. 'I see,' she said carefully. 'You're a confirmed bachelor, hmm?'

Gray's eyes narrowed. 'I like my freedom, yes. That's something a woman like you would understand, isn't it?'

Jeanne swallowed. 'Yes. Yes, of course.'

He puffed out his breath. 'Exactly,' he said, turning away from her and leaning his elbows on the low wall. 'Seth must give you as rough a time as Abigail gives me.' His head swivelled towards her. 'I mean, he wants to get you settled down, doesn't he? Married off to the right man?'

She sighed. 'I suppose.'

Gray nodded. 'He tells me you're an actress.'

She felt a stir of irritation. How much had Seth told this stranger about her, anyway?

'Not quite,' she said politely. 'Actually, just now, I'm a waitress.'

'A waitress. That must be a dull job for someone like you.'

Jeanne looked up sharply. There'd been something in Gray's voice—but he was looking at her blandly, an impersonal smile on his face.

Her shoulders slumped. 'It is,' she admitted. 'Some-times, I get so tired of——'

He turned and looked at her. 'An acting job would be better, wouldn't it? Something for the summer?'

Jeanne frowned. 'Of course. But they're not easy to come by.'

'What if someone offered you a job like that?'

'I don't understand.'

His eyes gleamed. 'What if you could get an acting job? An easy one. With good pay.'

'Here, you mean? In England? But that's impossible. I'd need a work permit. Besides, who'd offer me some-thing so——'

'I would.'

The easy good humour of the early morning was gone from Gray's voice. In its place was a cool triumph and, as Jeanne's eyes swept across his face, she saw that same exultation there as well.

'You? But you don't have anything to do with the theatre. You're in investments, like Seth.'

There was a pause, and then Gray spoke. 'I want you to pretend to fall in love with me.'

The cold precision of his words stunned her. She stared at him, searching for some sign that he was joking. But his eyes were fierce, his expression grim.

'What?' she whispered.

'I said, I want us to pretend to fall in love.' He spoke as calmly as if he'd suggested she become his typist. 'Oh, not right away, of course. We'll build up to it in stages.'

'You must be crazy!'

'What I need is a little diversion. I don't want to lie to Abigail on a grand scale.'

'A little diversion,' Jeanne repeated, her voice trembling.

Gray nodded impatiently. 'Yes. She'll do the rest herself—hope that things grow between us, that we decide to make our relationship permanent—but, when it's time for me to return to London, I'll simply tell her things didn't work out.'

Jeanne's hands clenched into fists. 'You're despicable! To think you'd do something so—so underhanded to that sweet old lady.'

His jaw thrust forward. 'Listen, little sister, I don't need any lectures from you. I love Abigail more than you can imagine.' His face grew dark as a thundercloud. 'I told you last night, she's ill. I'm not sure what will happen to her, if she's not careful. The only thing I'm certain of is that all this—this garbage she's into, the teas and dinners and lunches she arranges so she can trot every damned eligible female this side of the equator past me, wears her out.'

'Then tell her so. Tell her.'

'Save your advice, dammit!' His hands shot out and clasped her shoulders. 'I've tried telling her. I've tried everything—but there's no stopping her.' He drew in his breath. 'Nothing's ever stopped her—except you.'

Jeanne's eyebrows rose. 'Me? But . . .'

'Last night, when she realised you'd stay over, she backed out of the plans she'd made for this evening so fast it made my head spin.' His eyes grew dark. 'Apparently,' he said in a silken whisper, 'she thinks you'd be the perfect woman for me.'

Colour flared in her face. 'Well, she's wrong.'

Gray gritted his teeth. 'Absolutely. And if she knew the truth about you——'

'What truth?'

'Come on, Jeannie.' His mouth twisted until it was a thin line in his dark face. 'That innocent act won't work with me. It has Abigail fooled, and Seth. But you and I both know how things really are.'

Jeanne began to tremble. 'I was right about you all along,' she said. 'You're a bastard. A cold, hardhearted——'

His hands tightened on her. 'You can think I'm a savage with a bone through my nose, for all I care, just as long as you can play to an audience of one.'

'Let go of me.' Jeanne twisted against his hands. 'I said, let me go! I won't have any part of this.'

'What's the matter, little sister? Aren't you a good enough actress to pull it off?' A sly smile moved across his mouth. 'Hell,' he said softly, 'there might even be some interesting side benefits to the job, if we play our cards right.'

The sound of her hand slamming against his face echoed through the trees like a gunshot. Gray's breath hissed through his teeth; his face twisted, and Jeanne felt her mouth go dry with fear.

He looked like a man capable of anything.

They stared at each other for a long moment, and then he caught her wrist in his hand and began striding towards the house.

'What are you doing?' she demanded. 'How dare you?'

'What am I doing? I'm doing a favour for an old pal.' His voice was like ice as he tugged her along with him. 'Seth's got a right to know what his baby sister's been up to lately.' They crossed the meadow, to the house, and he opened a side door. A narrow staircase rose ahead, and Gray started up it. Jeanne had no choice but to stumble along after him.

'Where are you taking me, dammit?'

'To my rooms, so I can phone Seth in private.' His teeth flashed in a frigid smile as he drew her inside a small, pannelled study. The door swung shut behind them, and Gray let go of Jeanne's wrist.

She stared at him, her breasts heaving rapidly beneath her sweatshirt. She was shaking with anger—and fear, although she was determined not to let him know that.

'Good.' Her chin lifted. 'I'll talk to my brother, if you don't mind. I'm sure he'll want to know that his good old pal, Graham Caldwell, is a degenerate. And a bully. And——'

'Tell him anything you like,' Gray said softly. He reached past her to the telephone. 'But first I'll fill him in on little sister's behaviour the past few days. I'm sure he'll be fascinated.'

Jeanne shook her head. 'You wouldn't. He's your friend.'

'Right. That means I owe him the truth.' His mouth narrowed into a grim line. 'If you were *my* sister, I'd sure as hell want to know you were in the habit of falling into men's beds whenever the mood struck you.'

'He won't believe you.'

His smile chilled her. 'Want to bet?'

She stared at him, while a cold rage rose inside her. 'My brother trusts me.'

'Does he?'

Gray's voice twisted the simple question into the worst sort of accusation.

Jeanne's eyes locked with his. 'Give me the phone,' she said quietly. 'If anyone's going to tell Seth what's happened, it's going to be me.'

A muscle moved in his jaw. 'There's still a way out of this,' he said softly. 'All you have to do is agree to my terms. We can tell Seth you've decided to stay and be my aunt's companion until I can find someone permanent.'

'The phone,' she said coldly.

Gray uttered an oath and handed it to her. He watched as she placed the transatlantic call.

Her hands sweated as she heard the ring of the phone. It was still early morning back in Connecticut—why hadn't she thought of that? Seth and Kristin would still be asleep, they'd be frightened when they heard her voice.

'Hello?'

'Seth.' Jeanne closed her eyes and leaned back against the wall. 'Seth, I'm sorry to call at this hour. But——'

'What's the matter, Jeannie?' Her brother's voice was taut with concern. Kristin's sleep-thickened voice murmured softly in the background.

'Nothing. I just—I just...'

'Jeanne.' Seth's tone hardened. 'Have you gotten yourself into some kind of scrape again?'

'No,' she said quickly, 'of course not. I simply——'

'I might have known it,' he said grimly. 'I let you out of my sight for a couple of weeks, and——'

A coldness began seeping into her bones. 'That's very reassuring,' she said stiffly. 'Is that how you see me? As someone who needs watching over?'

Her eyes met Graham Caldwell's. He was laughing, damn him, he was laughing at her!

'Let's get to it,' the voice in her ear said. 'What have you gotten yourself into this time?'

Jeanne drew a deep breath. 'I called to tell you—to tell you...' She looked at Gray helplessly. 'I called to tell you,' she said carefully, 'that I won't be home the day after tomorrow.'

'What? This line is bad, Jeannie. It sounded as if you said——'

'I did.' She spoke quickly, almost slurring the words. 'Your friend, Graham Caldwell, has asked me to—to be his aunt's companion for the next couple of weeks, and I've agreed.'

The phone buzzed with silence, and then Seth cleared his throat.

'You've agreed?'

Jeanne nodded. 'Yes,' she whispered. 'I have. I—I'll let you know when I'm flying in, Seth.'

'Jeanne...'

'Give my love to Kristin, will you?'

She slammed down the phone and wrapped her arms around herself. Slowly, her head rose and her eyes met Gray's.

'Satisfied?' she asked in a bitter voice.

He smiled like a cat in a room filled with slow-witted mice. 'Very.'

Jeanne met his gaze as long as she could, and then she turned away, trembling.

What have you gotten yourself into this time? Seth had asked.

It was a damned good question.

CHAPTER SEVEN

WHEN she was little, Jeanne had holidayed in California with her family. They'd spent an exciting week in San Francisco, and then they'd driven down the coast highway to San Diego. Just outside Santa Barbara, her father had pulled to the side of the road so they could walk down to the beach and watch a family of dolphins cavorting in the sea—and suddenly the earth had shifted beneath Jeanne's feet.

'What's happening, Daddy?' she'd whispered, wide-eyed.

It was an earthquake. Not a big one; a minor earthquake, the sort that native Californians didn't even notice. But Jeanne had never forgotten the terrifying sensation that came of feeling the ground slip beneath you.

Clutching her father's hand, she had half expected a yawning chasm to open before her and swallow her whole.

It was how she felt now, as she slammed the door behind her and hurried down the stairs from Gray's panelled study.

Graham Caldwell had pushed his way into her life and changed a pleasant, if unexciting, vacation into something impossible.

Damn the man for doing this to her! How could he? How *dared* he? How...?

She paused at the foot of the stairs and slumped back against the wall.

Tell the truth, she thought. The man might be an unmitigated bastard, but she was as responsible for this mess as he.

95

It was her own stubborn pride that had done her in. Seth had taken the big brother tone he'd used so many times before, the one that made her feel ten years old, and she'd bristled. No. She'd done worse; she'd responded as if she were, in fact, ten years old, and now she was trapped.

Jeanne looked up the narrow staircase. But it was an easily sprung trap. All she had to do was go back and tell Gray she'd changed her mind.

'I won't be part of this insane charade,' she'd say. 'Even the thought of letting you touch me makes me shudder.'

Her jaw firmed. She took a step up and then a second, only to sag back against the banister.

It was a lie. God, it was a lie—and they both knew it.

She closed her eyes, remembering what had happened after she'd hung up the phone. She'd been standing with her back to Gray, trying to compose herself before she faced what she knew would be his look of triumph, when suddenly she'd felt the warmth of his hands on her shoulders.

'Don't,' she'd hissed.

But Gray had only laughed softly and drawn her back against his chest.

'Holding you will be part of the performance, Jeannie. How else will I convince my aunt?'

Jeanne spun around, eyes blazing.

'You'll never pull this off, you know. Abigail's not a fool.'

And Gray smiled, so knowingly and intimately that she felt her blood thicken.

'You're right,' he murmured. 'She's not.' His hands slipped from her shoulders to her wrists. Slowly, he raised her hands until her palms rested against his chest. 'So you're going to have to give the best performance of your life.'

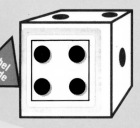

NO RISK, NO OBLIGATION TO BUY...NOW OR EVER!

GUARANTEED

PLAY "ROLL A DOUBLE" AND GET AS MANY AS FIVE GIFTS!

HERE'S HOW TO PLAY:

1. Peel off label from front cover. Place it in space provided at right. With a coin, carefully scratch off the silver dice. This makes you eligible to receive two or more free books, and possibly another gift, depending on what is revealed beneath the scratch-off area.

2. You'll receive brand-new Harlequin Presents® novels. When you return this card, we'll rush you the books and gift you qualify for ABSOLUTELY FREE!

3. Then, if we don't hear from you, every month, we'll send you 6 additional novels to read and enjoy. You can return them and owe nothing, but if you decide to keep them, you'll pay only $2.49 per book—a saving of 40¢ each off the cover price.

4. When you subscribe to the Harlequin Reader Service®, you'll also get our newsletter, as well as additional free gifts from time to time.

5. You must be completely satisfied. You may cancel at any time simply by sending us a note or a shipping statement marked ''cancel'' or by returning any shipment to us at our expense.

The Austrian crystal sparkles like a
diamond! And it's carefully set in a romantic
"Key to Your Heart" pendant on a generous
18″ chain. The entire necklace is yours free
as added thanks for giving our Reader
Service a try!

"ROLL A DOUBLE!"

PLACE LABEL HERE

SCRATCH HERE

?

**SEE CLAIM CHART
BELOW**

106 CIH AEK2
(U-H-P-04/92)

YES! I have placed my label from the front cover into the space
provided above and scratched off the silver dice. Please rush me
the free books and gift that I am entitled to. I understand that I am
under no obligation to purchase any books, as explained on the
opposite page.

NAME _____

ADDRESS _____ APT. _____

CITY _____ STATE _____ ZIP CODE _____

CLAIM CHART

⚅ ⚅	**4 FREE BOOKS PLUS FREE "KEY TO YOUR HEART" NECKLACE**
⚅ ⚄	**3 FREE BOOKS**
⚅ ⚁	**2 FREE BOOKS**

CLAIM NO.37-829

HARLEQUIN "NO RISK" GUARANTEE

DETACH AND MAIL CARD TODAY!

BUSINESS REPLY MAIL
FIRST CLASS MAIL   PERMIT NO. 717   BUFFALO, NY

POSTAGE WILL BE PAID BY ADDRESSEE

HARLEQUIN READER SERVICE
3010 WALDEN AVE
PO BOX 1867
BUFFALO NY 14240-9952

NO POSTAGE
NECESSARY
IF MAILED
IN THE
UNITED STATES

She could feel the heavy beat of his heart beneath her fingertips, and her heart began to race in response. But her voice, when she answered, was cold.

'It won't work, Gray.'

'It will, if we play things right.'

'I tell you, it won't work. This is the real world, not the theatre.'

His brows arched, and a sardonic smile curved across his lips. 'Are you saying you aren't capable of playing to an audience of one?'

'Why do you keep making it sound as if I'm at the heart of this? It's not me. It's——'

'You're right,' he said softly. She saw the sudden darkening in his eyes, and she took a step away, but not quickly enough. His arms closed around her, and he drew her slowly towards him again. 'I'll have to do my part, too.' His hands spread on her back, moulding her to him. 'And I will, Jeannie. You can count on it.'

'Jeanne,' she said idiotically. 'My name is——'

Gray laughed softly as he bent to her. 'Are you always so formal with your lovers?'

The air in the room seemed to grow thick. Suddenly, it was difficult to draw enough of it into her lungs.

'You're not my lover. And you never will be. I told you——'

His mouth dropped to hers. She struggled wildly at first, beating her hands against his chest, trying desperately to twist away from him. But she couldn't. He was too determined, too powerful—and then, oh, lord, and then...

And then, as she gave herself up to what was happening, she didn't want to end the kiss.

What had begun as a challenge changed. A slow heat began to build deep within her. Its warmth spread slowly through her veins, along her skin, and all at once, she was lost.

She moaned softly, and her lips parted to his. Her hands snaked up to his shoulders and spread over the

firm muscles that lay knotted beneath his still damp
sweatshirt. He whispered something against her mouth
and his arms gathered her closer until the hardness of
his body and the curving softness of hers were almost
one. His tongue thrust into her mouth, and the heat and
taste of him filled her.

The room, and the reality of why he had brought her
to it, spun away. Nothing mattered but the man in her
arms and the fire that was hell-bent on consuming them.

The kiss had gone on and on, until one of them—
Gray, she thought now, colour flooding her cheeks at
the realisation—until Gray had put her from him.

Her lashes had lifted slowly, and she'd stared at him,
her breath catching when she saw his face. Whatever
she'd expected to see, it was not this: his eyes as dark
as the midnight sky, a look in them she could not define.

A chill had swept over her skin. Anger. That was what
she'd seen in his face. No, not anger. Rage. But why?
He was the one who'd started this, he was the one
who'd . . .

And then it was gone, so swiftly that she'd told herself
she must have imagined it.

'You see?' His voice had been slow, almost a drawl,
and he'd smiled that easy smile of his as he ran his
knuckles lightly along her cheek. 'There won't be any
problem convincing my aunt. Will there, darling?'

His tone had made a mockery of the endearment.
Jeanne had stared at him in silence while she'd searched
desperately for something to say—some clever, cutting
remark that would tell him that the kiss had all been as
much a game to her as it had been to him—but her fe-
vered brain had become numb. She couldn't even imagine
a retort that would return control of the situation to her.

She'd made, at last, a gesture so theatrical it made
her cringe to remember it—she'd wiped the back of her
hand across her mouth, turned abruptly and exited the
room like a *grande dame* in a cheap melodrama.

Gray's soft laughter had followed her down the stairs.

The sound of it seemed to ring in her ears now, as she looked up the steps to his closed door. No, she thought as she turned and made her way down again, there was no sense in going back and confronting him. He would only laugh at her, or worse. He might take her in his arms again, turn her protests into soft whimpers of acquiescence.

There was a door just ahead. She pulled it open quickly, stepped through, then shut it after her. She was back in the library of Caldwell House, and not a moment too soon, she thought as she leaned back against the closed door. Her glance flew to the clock on the fireplace mantel. It was late; Abigail would be wondering what had...

'There you are, dear.'

Gray's aunt stood in the far doorway, smiling at her. Smile back, she told herself fiercely, smile back and say something.

'Good morning, Mrs Caldwell.'

The old woman clucked her tongue. 'Abigail, please. I thought I'd told you that last night.'

Jeanne nodded. 'You did,' she said. She drew a breath, then leaned away from the door. 'I guess I forgot.'

'Have you had breakfast yet? Cook can make whatever you—— '

'No,' Jeanne said quickly. The thought of food made her throat close. She smiled politely. 'I'm not much for breakfast.'

The old woman smiled in return. 'Well, we'll see if we can't change that, while you're with us these next two weeks.'

Jeanne stared at her. 'But how did you...?'

'Graham told me he was going to ask you to stay.'

'Did he?' Jeanne's voice was flat. 'Did he, really?'

'Yes. And I must say, I'm delighted.'

'I—I don't want to impose on your hospitality.'

'Nonsense. I'm looking forward to your company.' The elderly woman's eyes gleamed as she leaned forward. 'I'm so thrilled Graham wants you to stay.'

The women's gazes met. Overwhelmed by guilt, Jeanne looked quickly away.

'I wouldn't make too much of it,' she said cautiously. 'It's just—well, your nephew suggested I might want to extend my vacation.'

But Abigail wasn't listening. She was thumbing through a leather-bound appointment book.

'How does Friday evening strike you?'

Jeanne frowned. 'I'm sorry, Abigail. I'm afraid I'm not following you.'

Gray's aunt sighed. 'Forgive me, dear. I'm running ahead of myself.' She looked up, brows lifted. 'I thought it would be nice if you met some of Graham's friends. He spent summers here, when he was a boy. And, of course, he's been here ever so often during the past years.'

'Abigail.' Jeanne sat down beside her. 'I wouldn't want you to—to get the wrong idea about your nephew and me. We're—we've...'

'Just met. Of course.' Abigail's eyes twinkled. 'All the more reason you should meet his other friends, don't you think?'

'You mustn't put yourself to any trouble. Gray wouldn't...'

Abigail waved her hand in the air. 'I won't do a thing. I'll ask people to come by after dinner. Nancy can bake some cookies.' She smiled and patted Jeanne's hand. 'Actually, I'd already asked a few people to stop in— the Treadwells, up the road. And the vicar and his wife. A handful more won't hurt.' She looked at Jeanne. 'Unless,' she said hesitantly, 'you'd rather not meet our friends.'

'Of course I would,' Jeanne said quickly. 'But...'

Abigail patted her hand. 'The Archers,' she said, making a note in the appointment book. 'Oh, and the Darbys—although how can I ask them without asking their daughters?' She looked up, eyes dancing. 'I don't suppose you'd want to meet them, too, would you, dear?'

'The Darby sisters?'

'Graham dated them a few times when he was younger. They always find reasons to come round when he's here, the same as the Dietrich girl.' She chuckled. 'And if they don't, I invite them. But I won't this time, of course.'

Jeanne looked at her. All the women Gray had schemed so hard to avoid, she thought, and she smiled sweetly.

'But I'd like to meet them,' she said.

Abigail chuckled. 'Clever girl. It would give you some insight into Graham, wouldn't it?'

Jeanne leaned back and folded her hands in her lap. 'Something like that.'

'Well, then, why don't you hand me the telephone, and we'll get started?'

It was, Jeanne thought as she listened to Gray's aunt make the first of the morning's worth of calls, a small victory.

But it was a sweet one, none the less.

The days passed slowly, falling easily into a pattern that followed the example set by the first. Jeanne came down each morning to find Gray waiting for her.

'Good morning,' he'd say, she would nod in return, and then they would set off together, jogging down the lane, to the road, to the crossroads, then back.

She had objected, at first. But Gray had pointed out that Abigail expected it—she thought it was charming that the two of them had what she insisted on calling 'racing' in common. He pointed out, too, that jogging together was the easiest part of the deception.

It was true. With no one watching, there was no need to pretend. They ran in silence, sometimes not exchanging a word until they arrived back at the house again, but even there things were relatively uncomplicated.

Gray was kept busy the first few days, meeting with contractors and planning renovations to the house. The evenings were not as difficult as Jeanne had expected, either. The three of them dined together, talking of this and that, and then they went to the library for coffee. Gray read, while Jeanne and Abigail chatted.

Jeanne had almost begun to believe she might get through the remaining days without difficulty.

But on Friday, everything changed.

She and Gray were on the last leg of their jog, when suddenly he caught her arm and brought her to a stop.

'Look,' he said, pointing to the road ahead.

A large bird—a hawk, she saw—was bent over a road-kill. As she watched, the hawk grasped what was left of the dead creature in its talons, flapped its wings, and rose into the sky.

'How nice,' she said, while she fought to catch her breath.

Gray glanced at her in amusement. 'Well,' he drawled, 'that's one for the books. I doubt if most women would applaud that sight.'

Jeanne grinned. 'I'm from Colorado, remember? After living in New York all this time, I was beginning to think I'd never see anything but pigeons, starlings and sparrows again.'

He grinned, too, as they began jogging slowly down the road. 'Ah, yes, the curse of the cities.'

'You mean, London?'

'I mean, everywhere.' He laughed. 'Did Seth ever tell you about the time he and I met in Paris? No? Well, we'd discovered we'd both be there on business the same day, so we'd arranged to meet at the Café de la Paix for drinks, and then we had tickets for the opera. There we were, both of us dressed like advertisements for formal wear, strolling along the Champs Elysées on our way to the café, when suddenly we passed under what looked like a cloud of pigeons...'

Jeanne began to giggle. 'Poor Seth. Once, when we were in California on vacation, he took me to the aquarium. It was outdoors, and there were seagulls everywhere. And...'

By the time they got back to the house, they were both laughing. Abigail was waiting for them in the dining-room.

'Well,' she said brightly, 'you two look as if you've had a good time.'

Gray smiled. 'Jeannie and I were comparing notes about the wildlife in Paris and points west.'

His aunt's eyes widened. 'Wildlife?'

'Yeah.' He chuckled, and Jeanne did, too. 'It's kind of difficult to explain,' he said, draping his arm over Jeanne's shoulders. 'Isn't that right, Jeannie?'

She looked up at him, and they both grinned. 'Yes,' she said, 'I guess it is.'

They went on smiling at each other for a few seconds, and then Gray patted her lightly on the bottom.

'To the showers,' he said. 'Tell Nancy to keep the coffee warm, Auntie. We'll be down in a minute.'

On the upper landing, at the door to Jeanne's room, Gray caught her arm and turned her to him.

'You've a smudge of dirt on your face.'

Her hand went to her cheek. 'Where?'

'There.'

She caught her breath as he moistened his fingertip, then ran it lightly across her nose. The feel of his hand against her skin sent unexpected tingles of pleasure dancing down her spine.

When he'd finished, she gave him a shaky smile. 'Thanks.'

'You're welcome,' he said solemnly. 'In fact, anything I can do to help...' Jeanne looked at him, and laughter glinted in his eyes. 'Well, if there are any places you can't reach when you're in the shower, washing backs is my speciality.'

She stiffened for an instant, and then she laughed. Gray was watching her, his grin so open and good-natured that it was impossible to take offence.

It was friendly, teasing banter, nothing more, and only a fool would be insulted.

'You're a man of many talents, Mr Caldwell,' she said, tossing her head, and then she laughed, stepped into her room and closed the door gently in his face.

When she came downstairs a little while later, Abigail was reading the newspaper with her second cup of coffee.

'Graham's in the garden, dear. He said to take your coffee out and join him.'

She found him leaning against an ancient elm, staring up at the house.

'It needs a bit of paint,' he said by way of greeting.

Jeanne's gaze followed his to the upper-storey shutters. 'Will the contractor be starting work soon?'

'Next week. I'd have done it myself, but Abby would have been out here, supervising every inch of the way.'

Her eyebrows rose. 'You?'

Gray's teeth glinted in a quick smile. 'I'll have you know I'm one heck of a painter, Miss Lester.'

'I wouldn't have thought there was much call for painting in the London stock market,' she said drily.

He laughed. 'No, but it doesn't hurt to have some more basic talent to fall back on, when you deal in something as chancy as stocks and bonds.' He moved away from the tree, took her elbow, and led her to a white wrought-iron table and chairs that stood surrounded by Abigail's prize rose bushes. 'Actually,' he said, pulling a chair out for Jeanne, 'I knew how to wield a paintbrush long before I knew how to put together a packet of bonds.'

She smiled. 'I'll bet.'

'Cross my heart,' he said, sinking into the seat opposite. 'My father owns a construction company just outside Chicago. I worked for him all through high school and college—except for the times I was in the UK.'

She looked at him, her gaze moving over the tanned, muscled flesh, picturing him in her mind's eye as he must have looked then. He would have been a handsome boy, she thought, but not half as good-looking as he was now, with his body hardened and matured.

Their eyes met and Jeanne flushed and looked into her cup.

'Was your father English?'

Gray shook his head. 'My uncle was stationed in England during the war. He met Abigail, married her, and made a life here.'

'Didn't they have children?'

He shook his head. 'No. When he died, Abby was alone.' He smiled and took a sip of his coffee. 'When I decided to move to London, she just about adopted me.'

Jeanne smiled in return. 'She really loves you a lot, doesn't she?'

He sighed and leaned back in his chair. 'No more than I love her. But she won't slow down, and it worries me. And I can't convince her I don't need looking after.'

'I suppose she still thinks of you as a child,' Jeanne said. She put down her coffee and propped her elbows on the table, steepling her hands beneath her chin. 'I know what that's like.'

Gray leaned back in his chair, his eyes on her face. 'Do you?'

She nodded. 'My mother was a widow when she married my Dad. They had me later than usual—it was wonderful, in a way, because they had lots of time to devote to me. But it also meant I didn't get much chance to stand on my own feet.' She sighed as she traced her finger over the rim of her cup. 'As for Seth—he was ten when I was born, and he just seemed to take to the role of big brother naturally.' She smiled wistfully. 'Sometimes, it was like having three parents. "You can't do that, Jeanne,'' they'd say, when I wanted to try something different.'

Gray smiled a little. 'Something crazy, you mean.'

Jeanne looked at him. 'You sound as if you've been listening to Seth,' she said, tossing her head. 'No. Nothing crazy. Just different.'

'Such as?'

'Such as—I don't know. Learning to ride a motorcycle. Camping out alone. Building a rabbit hutch.'

His mouth twitched. 'A rabbit hutch?'

Her eyes met his, daring him to laugh. 'Yes. I wanted a rabbit. My mother said it would need a hutch, and where would I get one? I'd build it, I said.'

'You? Build a hutch?'

'You see? That was Seth's reaction, exactly. But I was determined. I scavenged wood and nails from everywhere, I sent away for the plans—and then I came home from school one day, and Seth had built the hutch for me.' She smiled sadly at the memory. 'I thanked him, of course. But I was so disappointed. I'd wanted to do the job myself.' Her voice faded, and then she laughed self-consciously. 'I don't know why I told you all that, Gray. I mean, it really doesn't matter that much now.'

'Maybe he was afraid you'd hurt yourself.' His voice roughened. 'You can't blame a man for wanting to protect you.'

Jeanne glanced up. Gray was watching her narrowly, all the laughter gone from his face.

'I'm not blaming him,' she said. 'You don't have to rush to his defence. It's just that I wish everyone would try letting me live my own life.'

'I thought they were.' His voice was flat. 'You live alone. You have an extraordinary career as a waitress.' A tight smile angled across his mouth. 'And, of course, we mustn't forget the men you've been involved with.'

So much for their short-lived truce, she thought, and she rose to her feet.

'I'll be in my room.'

'Jeanne.' Gray rose, too, and caught her hand as she started past him. 'I'm sorry. I've no right to judge what you do with your life.'

'You don't have to make any apologies to me,' she said stiffly.

'I do. And I am.' He smiled. 'I can't offer you a rabbit hutch, but will a bird-house do?'

She stared at him. 'What?'

'I've been meaning to repair the bird-house in Abby's garden. I thought you might like to help.'

Jeanne looked at him warily, searching his face for the coldness that had been there only moments ago. But his expression was open and pleasant.

'Do you mean it?'

He grinned. 'Who am I to deny a woman the chance to learn a new skill?'

They worked in companionable silence all afternoon. Abigail came out and watched them for a while, smiling as Gray steadied Jeanne's hand as she sawed a length of wood, nodding approval as she fitted the piece to the structure.

'You're a good team,' the old woman said at day's end, as she watched them put away the tools.

Jeanne flushed, but Gray put his arm around her waist and hugged her lightly to him.

'She's a good worker,' he said. He smiled, and then he dropped a kiss on the top of her head. 'She's full of surprises.'

His aunt smiled, too. 'Most women are.'

Jeanne looked up, and met Abigail's eyes. She felt a sudden stab of guilt: the party Abby had planned was tonight.

'Let's keep how many people I've invited a secret,' Abigail had suggested. 'Gray will probably balk if he knows. Why don't we tell him I've only asked a couple of neighbours for coffee?'

Jeanne had agreed readily, relishing the thought of his discomfort at finding himself surrounded by the women he'd schemed so hard to avoid.

Now, after the long, pleasant day they'd spent together, she regretted her silence. But there was still time to warn him, she thought as they went slowly up the stairs together, his arm still curved comfortingly around her.

She turned towards him when they reached her door. 'Gray, about this evening——'

'Just look at that,' he said, softly. 'There's a smudge on your face again.'

Jeanne frowned. 'Where?'

'On your mouth.' Before she could move, he lifted his hands to her face, framing it between them. Her heart skipped a beat as he leaned towards her. 'Right—there,' he whispered.

Her eyes closed as his mouth covered hers. She stood still for a moment, and then her hands rose and she linked them behind his neck. It seemed a long while later when he finally raised his head and smiled into her eyes.

'There,' he whispered. 'That wasn't so bad, was it?' He leaned back against the wall and took her with him. 'In fact, it was pretty nice.'

A little note of warning sounded, but she shut her heart to it.

'Yes,' she said. 'It was.'

'And it was a nice day, too, don't you think?' He drew her closer. 'Laughing together, talking, kissing me—see? You survived it all.'

'Survived?'

His eyes met hers. 'If our relationship's going to seem real, it has to develop.' A smile moved across his mouth. 'Surely you didn't think we'd stay at the friendship stage forever.'

Jeanne felt a coldness seeping into her veins. The meaning of his words, and his actions, suddenly became painfully clear.

Everything that had happened today—all of it, from start to finish—had been carefully planned. Gray had orchestrated a scenario to deceive his aunt. And she'd played her part in it, without even realising he'd contrived the whole thing.

Pain gripped her heart. How could she have been such a fool?

'You're right,' she said, stepping out of his arms. 'I survived.'

For a moment, she thought she saw something glint in the depths of his eyes, something that threatened to wipe away his smug, self-assured smile. But then his eyes narrowed, and he reached out for her again.

'I thought, since we'd made such good progress, you might like to move things along a little.'

A shiver moved along her skin. 'Meaning?'

'Meaning,' he said softly, 'this house has an antiquated plumbing system. Why use two showers when one will suffice?'

'I turned down that offer this morning,' she said calmly, although her heart was galloping. 'Why would you think I'd change my mind?'

The self-confident smile angled across his face again. 'This morning was different,' he said. He put his hand to her hair and stroked it gently back from her flushed cheeks. 'We know each other better now. Today was a kind of milestone, when you think about it. No arguments, no nasty words...'

'...and no substance.' Her smile was cool, and she saw the sudden change in Gray's face, the way his mouth hardened. Her chin lifted. 'I'm an actress,' she said. 'A good one. I thought you understood that.'

For a second, she thought she had pushed him too far.

'Listen,' he said, his voice gruff, 'I've had just about enough of your innocent act.' His eyes darkened. 'I'll be damned if I want the dubious honour of being the first man you've ever turned away.'

Jeanne reached behind her and turned the knob to her bedroom door. It opened slowly.

'Your aunt's expecting guests this evening, Gray. We wouldn't want her to have to greet them alone, would we?'

She stepped back, slipping into the room, closing the door on him before he could react, and then threw herself on the bed and buried her face in the pillow.

The entire day had been a lie, all of it an act they were putting on for Abigail, and the way he could make her respond when he took her in his arms only added a touch of reality to it.

Jeanne let out a sobbing breath. She would be safe as long as he thought it was an act for her, as well.

But it wasn't. Whatever she felt for Graham Caldwell had nothing to do with acting.

CHAPTER EIGHT

THE Waterford goblet rang as Abigail's salad fork brushed it gently, the delicate sound magnified by the silence of the dining-room so that it seemed as loud as the peal of a doorbell.

The elderly woman looked up and smiled in apology. 'Sorry.'

Jeanne managed a smile in return, but Gray only frowned.

'Are you all right, Abigail?'

'Yes, of course.' His aunt's brows rose delicately. 'Are you?'

His frown became a scowl. 'Certainly. Why do you ask?'

'I just wondered. You've been so quiet this evening.' The pale blue eyes went from her nephew's face to Jeanne's. 'The both of you, actually. I thought something might...'

Gray's lips drew back from his teeth. 'Jeanne and I had a long day, that's all. Isn't that right, Jeanne?'

The question was asked pleasantly enough. But the look that flashed across the table from beneath his dark lashes was an umistakable warning.

Her own eyes narrowed and focused on his, and then she turned to Abigail.

'If we did,' she said evenly, 'it's Gray's fault. He insisted on pushing things further than any reasonable man should.'

Gray's fork clattered against his plate. 'I don't think my aunt is interested in listening to this,' he said coldly.

'But it's true,' Jeanne said, her face a study in innocence. 'You were determined to get that bird-house fixed in one day.' She smiled. 'Isn't that right?'

111

She watched as his face darkened, and then, to her surprise, his expression changed and he began to laugh softly.

'You're just full of surprises, aren't you, little sister?'

'Yes,' she said softly. 'Maybe you should try remembering it.'

There was silence, and then Abigail cleared her throat. 'Well,' she said briskly, 'if you children are done eating...'

Jeanne tore her eyes from Gray's. 'Yes,' she said, barely glancing at the food lying untouched on her plate. 'Yes, thank you, I'm finished.'

Gray pushed his chair back and got to his feet. 'Aunt Abby,' he said. His aunt smiled as he helped her from her chair, and then she waved away his hand.

'Just give me my cane, please. That's the boy. Now. I've some things to discuss with Nancy, so you children take care of yourselves for a little while, all right?'

As soon as Abigail had limped from the room, Gray's face turned to stone. He swung towards Jeanne, hands on his hips.

'That was quite a performance you put on at dinner.'

Her brows rose. 'Was it?' she asked as she started past him. 'To tell you the truth, I thought it was rather pedestrian.'

His hand shot out and caught her wrist. 'Did you see my aunt's face? She knew something was wrong, dammit. People falling in love don't sit silent, staring into space, for the better part of an hour.'

Jeanne drew in her breath before she turned to face him. 'I told you this crazy scheme wouldn't work. But you were bound to go ahead with it just the same.'

Gray's jaw shot forward. 'If it's not working, the fault is yours, little sister. Every time I try to touch you——'

Two spots of colour appeared high on her cheeks. 'Don't call me that! I am not your sister.'

'You might as well be. Whenever I come too close, you act as if I were making an indecent proposal.'

'Which is exactly what you have been doing, ever since we met.'

His grip tightened on her wrist. 'Still,' he said, watching her face, 'it never takes much effort to change your mind, does it?' A tight smile angled across his mouth. 'After a few minutes in my arms, you always seem to forget just how much you despise me.'

His taunting words turned Jeanne's cheeks scarlet. He was trying to get a reaction from her, she knew. But she wasn't about to accommodate him. The memory of what had happened between them less than two hours ago was all too vivid.

Her smile was smoothly self-contained. 'I'd be lying if I didn't admit that you have a certain raw appeal.'

Gray's eyes darkened. 'Just what is that supposed to mean?'

Jeanne forced herself to meet his eyes. 'It means,' she said, 'that I can understand that a woman might find you attractive—if she likes the type.' She paused. 'Just don't make the mistake of taking my response too personally.'

She cried out as his grip tightened, and he pulled her closer. 'I see,' he whispered. 'Hell, I guess I should be flattered. How am I, compared to the other men you've known, Jeannie? Or would you like more data before you can come to any conclusions?'

'Let go of me, Gray.'

He smiled coldly. 'Make me.'

'Gray, damn you——'

There was a discreet cough from the doorway. They turned quickly to where Abigail Caldwell stood. She was watching them with a puzzled smile on her face.

Jeanne swallowed. 'Abigail.' Her eyes flashed to Gray's, met and held them, and he let go of her wrist.

'Aunt Abby.' Jeanne watched as he brought himself under control, then he turned slowly towards the old woman. 'Jeanne and I were just—we were talking about the guests you've invited for the evening. Who did you say was stopping by? The vicar?'

Abigail's eyes glinted mischievously. 'Well, actually, Graham, I asked some other friends in to meet Jeanne. Don't look at me that way,' she said. 'I promise, I've planned a simple evening. And I haven't lifted a hand. Mrs Jacobs baked cookies yesterday, and Jeanne was kind enough to make the punch this morning.'

His eyes narrowed as he looked at Jeanne. 'How nice.' After a moment, he turned to his aunt again. 'And who have you invited?'

His aunt pursed her lips, then rattled off a list of names. 'Oh, yes,' she said with a little glance at Jeanne, 'I asked the Darbys, too. And Sally Dietrich. Don't scold me, Graham,' she said quickly. 'They're such nice girls, and they always ask after you. And Jeanne said she wouldn't mind. Didn't you, dear?'

Gray glowered across the room. 'Is that what you said, *dear*?'

She lifted her chin. 'Yes.'

He stared at her through hooded eyes, and then he let out his breath. 'Why not?' His voice was silken, but somehow the sound raised the hairs at the nape of her neck. 'It should make for an interesting evening.'

Gray smiled at both women, then excused himself from the room. As soon as he'd left, Abigail motioned Jeanne to her side.

'I just know we're going to have a lovely time,' she said, linking their arms together. 'Graham didn't even grumble when I told him I'd invited the Darbys and Sally Dietrich.' She smiled happily. 'It's having you around that's done it, dear. You've been such a good influence on him.'

Jeanne sighed. 'Abigail,' she said gently, 'I wouldn't want you to—well, to expect too much from Gray and me.'

'You were having words when I came in a few minutes ago, weren't you? Don't look so distraught, dear. It's perfectly normal for people to quarrel once in a while.' The softly painted lips curled up in a smile. 'Especially if they care about each other.'

'You don't understand. Gray and I don't—we don't...'

She paused helplessly. Abigail was watching her with bright-eyed curiosity. How could she destroy all the old woman's illusions, especially on a night when she was so happy?

She sighed again and put her hand over Abigail's. 'I can hardly wait to meet your friends,' she said gently.

'And they can't wait to meet you. I know you're just going to love them all.'

An hour later, Jeanne was helplessly lost in a sea of names and faces. She had, over the past days, lost track of the number of people Abigail had invited, although she'd had a suspicion that the names she'd rattled off to Gray hadn't been a complete list.

Now, as she smiled politely and tried to imprint yet another face in her mind, she understood why Gray had been less than delighted with his aunt's attempts at entertaining. What Abigail had insisted would be a 'simple evening' seemed to have become instead a full-scale party.

The parlour was crowded with people. It was a warm night, and the french doors stood open, which was a good thing because the overflow crowd had spilled out into the garden and along the winding path that led through the property surrounding Caldwell House.

'Are you sure the excitement's not too much for you?' she'd heard Gray ask his aunt softly a little while ago.

Abigail had laughed and patted his cheek. 'I'm having a marvellous time, Graham,' she'd said. 'You just look after Jeanne.'

But it wasn't necessary. And that, Jeanne thought, as she stood in the centre of a small group of chattering matrons, was the best thing about the evening so far.

Gray had stayed beside her, at first, his arm lying lightly around her shoulders, although she had felt as if the weight of it might be more than she could bear.

'This is Jeanne Lester,' he'd say, and he never had the chance to add another word.

'From America,' someone would say, smiling and offering a handshake.

'Your friend's sister,' someone else would add. 'How nice.'

'And you've brought her for a visit.' This was almost always accompanied by a knowing smile. 'Isn't that lovely?'

And Gray would smile modestly, as if he had, in fact, brought her to his aunt's home for a visit, and Jeanne would smile, too, lending veracity to a myth that seemed to be growing before her very eyes.

'Gray's girl,' she heard someone whisper. 'Who'd have ever thought he'd settle down?'

'How can you do this?' she hissed to him when they were alone for a moment.

'Do what?' he said, smiling at her as if she were whispering something soft and intimate instead of condemning him with her eyes.

'Fool all these nice people. And your aunt—she's so happy tonight. What will you tell her when she learns the truth?'

Gray shrugged his shoulders. 'I haven't lied to anyone. They've all been eager to leap to their own conclusions.' He looped his arm around her waist and smiled at her again. 'There's Dr Ethridge. I'm sure he'd like to meet you.'

'Well, he'll just have to wait,' Jeanne said stiffly. She moved out of his encircling arm. 'Abigail's waving to me. I'm going to go talk to her for a while.'

It was the last she'd seen of Gray. No, she thought, glancing across the room, that wasn't quite accurate. She'd gone on seeing him—there he was now, laughing with a couple of men who'd been introduced to her as his boyhood chums. What had ended was his constant attendance on her, and thank heaven for that.

It was far easier to drift from group to group on her own, without Gray's hand on hers or the feel of his arm curved around her shoulders. His presence beside her was—it was too upsetting, it reminded her that she was here under false pretences.

Everyone in the room thought she and Gray were—were... She could see it in their smiles, hear it in their voices. And it was an assumption that angered her. The deception in itself was bad enough, but what was even worse was that the people in this room thought that she could ever care for a man like Graham Caldwell.

A peal of musical laughter drifted towards her. Jeanne glanced across the room. Gray had been standing beside the fireplace the last time she'd seen him, deep in conversation with a serious-looking gentleman dressed in tweed.

He was still in the same place. But now he was chatting with a young woman, someone who must have just arrived and who looked as out of place in this homey gathering as an orchid would among thistles. She was tall and willowy, and she had a shiny fall of platinum hair that swung over her shoulders each time she moved.

And she moved a lot. She was a study of grace in motion as she spoke to Gray, leaning towards him, putting her hand on his arm, then tossing her head back and laughing again.

Gray threw his head back and laughed, too.

He had, Jeanne thought suddenly, a nice laugh. It was open and warm, it made you feel as if whatever you'd said to earn it was special. He had laughed with her, this afternoon, when she'd told him about the rabbit hutch, and it had made her feel as if sharing her secret with him had been the right thing to do.

The woman smiled and put her hand on his arm again. Gray said something, then covered her hand with his.

Something knotted in Jeanne's stomach.

'...so very glad to meet you.'

She blinked and looked around. Abigail had come up beside her, arms linked with two pretty young women.

'I'm sorry,' she said, looking from one face to the other. 'What did you say, Abigail?'

'I said, Emily and Charlotte want to meet you, dear.' Gray's aunt smiled. 'These are the Darby sisters, Jeanne. They're very old friends of Graham's.'

The Darbys looked like twins, except that one was smaller and plumper than the other. It was she who held out her hand and smiled politely.

'How do you do, Miss Lester? I'm Emily Darby.'

'And I'm Charlotte,' the other girl said. 'It's a pleasure to meet you at last. We've heard so much about you.'

It was not a pleasure at all, Jeanne knew. The way they glanced from her to Gray told her so.

For an instant, she longed to tell them that they had nothing to worry about.

It's all a lie, she wanted to say. Graham Caldwell means nothing to me.

But her gaze followed theirs. Gray and the blonde were still together. They were walking towards the french doors now, Gray's dark head bent towards her fair one, his hand lying lightly on her shoulder.

The knot in Jeanne's belly tightened.

'Well,' Abigail said brightly. 'I'll just leave you girls to get acquainted, shall I?'

Jeanne looked at her helplessly, but the old woman smiled and melted into the crowd. Charlotte Darby cleared her throat.

'Have you been to England before, Miss Lester?'

'No. No, this is my first trip. And, please, call me Jeanne.'

'Has Graham shown you around Warwickshire?'

Jeanne shook her head. 'No, not really. We—we...' Her glance went to the french doors. The outside lights had been turned on as the evening darkened. She could just see Gray and the woman standing within their golden halo. They were facing each other now, and they were talking again. The woman's head was tilted back, she was looking up at Gray. It was easy to see that she was hanging on his every word.

Jeanne cleared her throat and looked at Emily Darby. 'Sorry. What were you saying?'

'I was asking if you thought you might be free one afternoon next week. Charlotte and I would love to have you to tea.'

Jeanne looked at the girl. The invitation was more than a polite gesture, she knew. It was an admission that she had won, and the sisters had lost.

She felt a stab of guilt. 'You've known Gray a long time, haven't you?'

Emily nodded. 'Ever since we were children.'

Jeanne drew a deep breath. 'I wouldn't—I wouldn't put too much stock in all this,' she said in a rush.

Charlotte frowned. 'In all what?'

Jeanne moistened her lips. 'In all—in...' Her eyes went to the french doors. Gray and the blonde were still there, centred in the garden lights like characters in a stage set.

The Darby sisters followed her gaze, and they sighed. 'In all that, you mean,' Emily said. She smiled. 'No, we don't. Sally's been playing that silly little game for years, but Gray's never really been impressed. Anyway, you're in his life now, Jeanne, aren't you?'

'Sally? Sally Dietrich?'

'Yes. The blonde with Graham now. Pretty, isn't she?'

Jeanne stared openly at the garden. As she watched, Gray put his arm around the blonde woman's shoulders and they began strolling along the path. Within seconds, the darkness swallowed them.

The knot in her belly became a stone that now seemed to lay lodged just under her heart.

She looked at Emily Darby, who was watching her with a puzzled expression on her face. She knew she must be making herself look foolish: she was having trouble keeping up her end of the conversation, and she kept turning away as if she were bored.

But she was not. She was—she was—dear heaven, what was she?

Gray had left her alone all evening. Wasn't that what she wanted?

He had been cornered by one of the very women he'd been trying so hard to escape.

Well, wasn't that what she'd wanted, too?

If Sally Dietrich had him in her clutches, it was no less than he deserved. She wanted him to suffer for the humiliation he'd heaped on her, for the way he'd bullied her into this masquerade. He was despicable. He was hateful.

Then why was she staring blindly into the darkness, wondering where he and the woman had gone? Why was she envisioning all the hidden crannies in Abigail's garden, spaces just the right size for two people who wanted a moment's privacy?

'Excuse me,' she said suddenly, giving the sisters a dazzling smile. Abigail waved gaily as she set off purposefully across the room. She waved back, but her thoughts were on the garden, the night, and the man and woman alone out there, somewhere in the quiet darkness.

Jeanne stepped out of the door and stood still while she got her bearings. People chatted quietly in little groups under the pool of light that lay just outside the house. Beyond, she could see nothing but blackness.

A woman smiled and touched her shoulder. 'We're leaving now, Miss Lester. It's been lovely meeting you. You and Gray will come and visit, won't you?'

Jeanne nodded, smiled, made a polite response. People were drifting off; it was getting late.

She stepped out slowly along the path. There was a murmur of voices ahead, and the sudden glow of a cigarette. A woman's voice rose in a soft trill of laughter.

'...the most fun, Gray. You should have been there. We'd have had such a good time together.'

The moon was rising. In its cold light, she could see Gray and the woman just ahead. They were standing beside the reflecting pool, close together. Gray's jacket was draped around her shoulders. For some reason, the sight of it hanging over that slender frame brought a coldness to Jeanne's heart.

She drew a deep breath, then walked towards them. 'Gray,' she said pleasantly. The couple turned swiftly. She caught a quick glimpse of the woman's face and the surprise mirrored there, and her chin rose. 'There you are, darling,' she said. 'I've been looking all over for you.'

Gray's face was still in shadow. It was impossible to see what effect, if any, her words had on him. Jeanne smiled as she reached his side. Easily, almost lazily, she put her hand lightly on his arm. 'Aren't you going to introduce us, darling?'

'Of course, Jeanne, this is Sally Dietrich.' What was it she heard in his voice? Was it amusement? 'Sally is— a very old friend.'

Yes. It was amusement. Thinly veiled laughter. Jeanne moved closer to his side and curled her hand around his bicep.

'How nice to meet you, Sally. I've been so looking forward to it.'

She held out her other hand. After a pause, the girl took it and shook it limply.

'Have you?' Her voice suited her cool blonde looks.

Jeanne nodded. 'Yes, indeed.' She drew her hand back and linked it with the other so that she was holding Gray's arm with both hands. 'In fact, that's what I told

Gray when we discussed tonight's guest list.' She felt his arm jerk under her fingers, and she smiled: ' "I'm not sure we should invite Sally," he said, but I insisted.' Her voice dropped to a purr. 'Men are so silly sometimes, aren't they? They just don't understand women at all.'

Sally drew in her breath, then let it out sharply. 'No. You're right, they don't.' She glanced up at Gray. 'For instance, I was just telling Gray how sweet it is that he's been so kind to his friend's little sister. Not all men would be bothered, would they?'

The women's eyes met. Sally's glittered with something hard and cold.

'Actually,' Jeanne said, leaning her head against Gray's shoulder, 'Gray didn't know who I was when we met.' She looked up at him. 'Didn't you tell Sally about that, darling?'

His brows rose. 'No. No, I didn't.'

She smiled. 'We met quite by accident, you see. Gray—well, I suppose it's all right to tell you, considering that he knows you so well—Gray tried to pick me up.'

God! Why was she saying these things? In the light of the moon, she saw a strange look in Gray's face. How delighted he must be with how well she was playing her role.

Stupid. She was being stupid. Sally Dietrich wanted the man, and she was welcome to him. She was...

'...back to the States?'

Jeanne wet her lips. 'Sorry, Sally. I didn't quite get that.'

'I said, when are you going home?' The sculpted mouth coiled into a smile. 'Don't you have a job or something to get back to?'

'Gray?' Jeanne looked up at him. 'It's gotten cool out here, darling. I see you've already given Sally your coat.'

'Yes. Would you like me to get you a wrap?'

He *was* laughing. Not so anyone could see it, no. But it was in his eyes, in his voice.

'No need to bother. Your arm around me would do nicely.'

His arm curved around her and he drew her close against him. She felt the heat of his body warming hers, and she realised that she had, in truth, been cold until he'd taken her into his embrace. She had never felt this warm, never.

'Isn't that right, love?'

Gray was smiling at her, his smile as intimate as it had been the day they'd met, when he'd asked her to go with him to The Swan and Rose.

What if she had gone? What if she had followed the crazy desire that had spiralled through her? What if she'd gone into his arms and his bed and never questioned anything else?

He drew her more tightly into the hardness of his body. 'I said, we're not sure when you'll be returning to the States. Isn't that right, Jeannie?'

Jeanne swallowed drily. Stop this, she thought desperately. Stop this now, before it goes any further.

'Actually,' she said, 'I've been thinking about that.'

His smile flickered. 'Have you.'

It was not a question, it was a warning. But she had to end this insanity before—before...

'Yes.' She forced herself to meet his gaze without flinching. 'I really must get home soon.'

Sally's smile returned, flashing on like a thousand-watt bulb. 'How unfortunate.' She clasped the lapels of the jacket draped around her shoulders. Her nails, Jeanne saw, were painted bright crimson. They looked like the bloodied talons of a predatory bird.

'Do phone me, Gray, when all your duties are completed and things are back to normal.' She tilted her head back so the shining platinum hair rippled in the moonlight. 'I think it was last summer, one of my little cousins came to visit for a few weeks—I had to take her everywhere.' The smile blazed on again, even more brilliantly.

'Castles and museums, that sort of thing. It was such a bore.'

'Was it?' Jeanne said. The sound of her own voice horrified her. Was she really speaking, or had she turned into a ventriloquist's dummy? 'We haven't had much time for touristy things.' Sally and Gray were both looking at her now, Sally with a frown and Gray with a smile that sent a whisper of pleasure dancing along her spine.

She smiled back. 'We've been dancing. And to the Lygon Arms, for dinner. And to all those cosy little pubs...' She was improvising wildly. She looked up at Gray again, startled to see that his expression had changed. There was a harshness in his face as he watched her, an angry twist to his mouth.

Suddenly, her voice—and her courage—failed her. What was she doing, anyway? She felt the sharp, unexpected pressure of unshed tears and she looked towards the reflecting pool.

'It's getting late.' Gray's voice was gruff. Jeanne tried to step away from him, but his arm tightened around her. 'You won't mind if I don't see you to the door, Sally?'

The Dietrich woman stared at him, and then she shook her head. 'No. No, of course not.' She looked at Jeanne, then quickly away. 'I'll just leave your jacket in the house, shall I?'

'That's fine. Goodnight, Sally.'

'I'll see you around, then, Gray.'

She strode off, heels clicking on the flagstones, head held high, and they were alone. A breeze from the meadow blew across the garden. Jeanne shivered under its touch.

'You *are* cold.'

Gray's voice was low, close to her ear. The whisper of his breath against her skin made a tremor go through her, and he turned and put both his arms around her.

'No,' Jeanne said quickly. 'I'm not cold. I just—I think it's probably time I went inside. It really is late—I don't hear any more voices. All your friends have probably...'

The nervous words trailed away. Gray was watching her, his expression closed.

'That was one hell of a performance.'

Jeanne looked at him. Was he angry? No. He couldn't be. She had done exactly what he'd wanted—hadn't she?

'I told you, I'm a good actress. You should have believed me.'

His arms tightened around her. 'How did you know Sally and I were out here?'

'I saw you,' she said, and then she caught her bottom lip lightly between her teeth. 'I mean, I just happened to notice that—that...'

'That I was taking her out into the garden for some air.'

The thick branches of an ancient oak caught the moon and held it captive. Darkness surrounded them, leaving Gray's face in shadow. If only she could see him, she thought. If only she could read something in his eyes.

'Look, there's no mystery to any of this.' Jeanne swallowed drily. 'I knew that the purpose of this whole exercise was to keep the sharks away.'

'The sharks?'

'You know what I mean. Sally, and the Darbys... And so, when I saw you out here with her, I just—I thought I'd just...' She broke off helplessly. 'Dammit, Gray, why are you making me explain?' She put her hands against his chest and tried to push him away. 'I'm going inside. Your aunt will be looking for us.'

'You're telling me you made Sally look like an opportunistic bitch for my sake. Is that right?'

Jeanne's head came up sharply. 'It didn't take much doing. But if I overstepped my bounds...'

'There was no other reason, is that what you're saying?'

There was. Of course, there was. The very sight of that pale blonde head next to his dark one, the proprietorial touch of Sally's hand on Gray's arm—there had been lots of reasons. There had been...

Gray shifted his weight and brought her closer against him, his hands slipping down her spine until they rested lightly on her hips.

'After all, you're just acting a role,' he said in a silken whisper. 'Isn't that so, Jeannie?'

She stared up at him, searching desperately for an explanation that would make sense, not just to him but to herself.

'Yes,' she said. 'Yes, exactly.' Her voice seemed even more husky than usual. 'I—I'm a method actress. Do you know what that means? I believe in the roles I play. I become one with my character.'

He laughed softly. 'I think you're lying, little sister. I think you saw Sally and me and you were jealous.'

Jeanne's mouth went dry. 'This is a ridiculous conversation. And don't call me by that silly name.' She tried to turn away, but his hands gripped her tightly. 'I want to go in now,' she said carefully. 'So if you don't mind...'

'All that nonsense about the places we've been together. What was that all about?'

'Look, if I interrupted something out here, I apologise. I was just doing what you——'

'Telling her we'd been out to dinner, that we'd been dancing, that we'd gone to all those cosy pubs.' The moon escaped the branches of the oak as he bent towards her, and she could see anger glint in his eyes. 'Lies, all lies. We haven't been out of that damned house. Not once.'

He was angry. More than angry. He was furious. A cold fist clamped around her heart as she realised that she'd spoiled his fun. It was just too bad that she hadn't understood his intentions earlier. Sally as husband hunter was one thing, but Sally as an available female was quite another.

Anger, as swift and consuming as his, rose within her. Was there no end to the ways Gray Caldwell intended to use her?

'You should have told me you wanted Sally as a playmate,' she snapped, twisting free of him. 'I'd have played my part differently.'

Gray's hand shot out and clamped around her wrist. 'Just listen to yourself,' he said tightly. 'Playmates, roles—children's games. Anyone would think that's all you know.'

'Let go of me, damn you!'

His face twisted as he stepped closer. There was a feral quality to him, one that sent a shudder of warning fluttering along her spine.

'But you only behave like a child when it suits you.' His breath quickened. 'Well, it doesn't suit *me*. Not any more.'

'I don't know what you're talking about.'

He laughed. 'Like hell you don't.' She cried out as he forced her arm behind her and her body was thrust forward in an arc against his. 'The Little Miss Innocent act is cute. Very cute.' Her breath caught as he moved his hand over her, stroking her from throat to breast with a touch that was as impersonal as it was shocking. 'I'll bet it's driven the other men you've known wild.'

Tears of rage rose in her eyes and she blinked them back. 'I hate you,' she hissed, the breath sobbing in her throat as his hand caressed her again. 'I hate you, Gray Caldwell, I despise you.'

His mouth dropped to hers with a ferocity that made her cry out in panic. She felt the scrape of his teeth, the hot thrust of his tongue.

Jeanne twisted her head away. 'I'll scream. Damn you to hell, I'll——'

He groaned as his arms closed around her and he kissed her again, his lips hard on hers, demanding her penance—and then, all at once, his kiss became a flame that intensified to a molten heat that was enough to sear her flesh and brand her as his, and only his, until the end of time.

Jeanne moaned and looped her arms around Gray's neck, pressing her body to his as he gathered her to him, tightly, tightly, until she knew without question that he was as aroused as she, that he wanted her as she wanted him.

His hands slid to her breasts and cupped them. Shock rippled through her as she felt her nipples harden in response. His thumbs moved over the silk of her gown as her body strained against his.

'I want you,' he whispered against her mouth.

She sighed his name, the hushed sound lost in the dizzying pleasure of his kiss.

'Oh, my goodness!'

Abigail's shocked voice drove them apart. They stared at each other, then swung towards the old woman. She looked from one flushed face to the other, and then she cleared her throat.

'I—I didn't mean to interrupt,' she said. 'I—er—I just wanted to say goodnight . . .'

Her voice tapered away. She smiled uncertainly, and then she turned and walked quickly towards the light.

Gray turned towards Jeanne.

'Jeannie,' he whispered.

But it was too late. She was already racing past him and into the house.

CHAPTER NINE

JEANNE awoke late, after having spent most of the night twisting sleeplessly in her bed. Shaken and humiliated, she had longed for the oblivion of sleep. Instead, her mind had played cruel tricks, forcing her to remember what had happened in the garden with exact—and devastating—precision.

Her eyes closed as the memories came sweeping back again. The heat of Gray's mouth, the heat of his hands—and the coolness of his eyes, that hard, knowing smile—she would never forget any of it. Never.

Gray had made love to her in a fierce maelstrom of rage and desire. He had touched her with fire but not with warmth. And she—God, she had responded with a passion as wild as his.

Jeanne flung the bedcovers aside and got to her feet. How could she have let it happen? How *could* she? George had loved her, Charlie had claimed to, but she'd never succumbed to their caresses or kisses. How could she have been caught in a dizzying spiral of desire with a man like Gray Caldwell, a man who'd used her, who thought the worst of her?

She padded barefoot to the window and drew back a corner of the curtain. Sunlight lay splashed across the garden, dappling the reflecting pool with streaks of brilliance. She'd stood this same way after fleeing to her room last night, watching Gray standing motionless where she had left him.

Suddenly, he had turned and lifted his head. The moon, riding in the dark sky, had made his face a harsh mask of shadowed planes and angles.

Jeanne had felt the air rush from her lungs. He couldn't see her, she'd told herself. But when, after a moment, Gray strode towards the house, she'd begun to tremble. Her ears had strained for the faint sound of the french doors closing after him, then for his tread on the stairs. He was coming to her, coming *for* her, and there would be no denying him this time.

The sound of her own pulse was like the beat of a drum in her ears. She'd shrunk back against the wall, watching the closed bedroom door, waiting...and finally his shadow had fallen across the sill. The world had dropped away from her, and vertigo had swept over her in a dizzying rush.

She'd held her breath, expecting the slow turn of the doorknob. But after an eternity of waiting, the shadow had disappeared and Gray's footsteps had sounded on the steps. She'd heard the snick of the front door closing, then the faraway growl of a car engine, and she knew he'd driven off into the night.

Jeanne turned from the window. He had come in hours later, when the promise of dawn had begun to tinge the night sky. She'd still been awake, staring into the darkness.

Where had he been? And who had he been with? Sally Dietrich, perhaps. Some willing woman, one who had lain in his arms, eager to meet his passion with her own?

A whimper rose in her throat. The question still plagued her now, although she told herself it was none of her business. Gray could do as he liked, and so could she. And what she was going to do now, this very day, was leave this house forever.

Tomorrow, she would be back in New York, and everything that had happened here would be nothing but a memory.

She dressed quickly in her usual early morning outfit of shorts, T-shirt, and running-shoes. It was late for their daily run, but the house was very quiet. Jeanne's mouth turned down. Gray had had a long night. Perhaps he'd slept in, too.

Not that she was in any mood for running or even for seeing him this morning. But she didn't want to hurt Abigail with an unexplained departure, and she knew Gray wouldn't want that either. No matter what else he was, he was devoted to the old woman. Between them, she and Gray could surely come up with a plausible excuse to justify her leaving.

Jeanne paused at the foot of the steps, listening for even the faintest sound. Puzzled, she glanced at her watch. Where was everybody? By now, she should have been able to hear the buzz of voices and the clatter of breakfast china.

Mrs Jacobs looked up from her recipe files as Jeanne pushed open the kitchen door.

'Good morning,' Jeanne said. 'Where is everybody?'

'Morning, Miss Lester. Nancy's upstairs, with Miss Abigail.'

'And Gray—Mr Caldwell?'

The woman shrugged. 'I dunno. Would you like some coffee?'

Jeanne looked across the kitchen. The percolator was bubbling gently on the stove. Her glance went to the coffee machine, sitting untouched on the counter. Only Gray used it—he called its strong, dark brew his American lifeline—but it was obvious he had not used it today.

Jeanne's heart did a strange tumble. Maybe Gray had simplified things for the both of them—maybe he'd risen early and left the house so that they wouldn't have to face each other this morning.

It certainly would make things easier, not seeing him again. Then why did the possibility distress her so? Why was there this sudden emptiness deep inside her breast?

'Miss Lester?' Jeanne blinked. The cook was watching her with a polite smile. 'Shall I pour you some coffee?'

She drew in her breath, then shook her head. 'No, no thank you. I—I——'

Behind her, the door swung open and banged against the wall. Jeanne turned quickly and came face to face with Gray. But this wasn't the Gray she knew: it was a glowering stranger, impeccably attired in a grey, pin-striped suit, white shirt, and dark tie.

'Where the hell have you been?'

'And good morning to you, too,' she said coolly.

He brushed past her as he strode across the kitchen, his glower deepening as he took the coffee-pot from the stove and filled a cup with its pale contents.

'This,' he said to Mrs Jacobs, 'is not coffee.'

'As you say, sir. Shall I...?'

Gray shook his head as she reached for the American coffee-machine. 'What for? So you can prove that it's possible to make two bad pots of coffee in one day?'

The woman flushed. 'I'm sorry, Mr Caldwell.'

Gray looked at her, then set down his cup and patted her arm. 'I'm sorry, too, Anna. I'm just—I'm...' He thrust his hand into his hair and turned towards Jeanne, who'd been watching his performance in silence. 'Abigail's ill,' he said brusquely.

'Ill?' she repeated stupidly.

'Yeah.' He leaned back against the counter and dug his hands into his trouser pockets. 'Nancy's with her now.'

'Sir?' Cook cleared her throat apologetically. 'I was just going off to do the shopping. Is that all right?'

'Yes. Yes, of course.' He waited until the woman had closed the kitchen door behind her, and then he looked at Jeanne. 'I didn't mean to bark at you,' he said. 'I'm just concerned about Abigail.'

'But what's wrong with her? Is it serious?'

He sighed. 'It's nothing, she says. But she always says that.'

'Always? You mean, this has happened before?'

He nodded. 'They aren't anything new. She gets these dizzy spells from time to time. Well, we'll see when the doctor gets here. I phoned him a little while ago.'

Jeanne moistened her lips with the tip of her tongue. 'Was it—is she ill because...?' He stared at her, watching as the colour rose swiftly into her face. 'It's not because she saw us, is it?'

He stared at her, and then comprehension dawned in his eyes. The lines around his mouth eased.

'I doubt it,' he said drily. 'We were kissing, Jeanne, not ravishing each other.'

'It was the party, then.' Jeanne pulled a chair from the table and sank into it. 'She kept promising she wouldn't do any of the actual work. She was so determined...'

Gray nodded. 'I can imagine.'

'And I should have told you that she was planning something larger than you thought.'

He looked at her. 'I wouldn't have missed that party for the world,' he said carefully. 'Such an interesting group of people, don't you think?'

Jeanne's eyes met his, then flew away. 'It's my fault she's ill,' she said, ignoring the challenge.

'Don't be ridiculous. It would take a directive from heaven itself to change Abby's mind, once she's set on something.' He smiled. 'My uncle used to say it was rather like trying to stop a charging elephant. You can either make a stand and get trampled, or live through it by getting the hell out of the way.'

A faint smile played over Jeanne's lips. 'Yes. I guess that's a pretty apt description.'

'Besides, if it hadn't been the party, it would have been something else. She tends to overdo.'

'Then—you think she'll be all right?'

He smiled. 'Now that I've had time to think about it, yes. I'm sure she will.' His smile broadened. 'Dr Ethridge will stop by this morning, tell her to take some pills and get plenty of rest, give me a look from under his brows that says she's impossibly stubborn, and have his office send me an exorbitant bill for confirming what everybody already knows.' He laughed softly, and the remaining lines of tension eased from his face. 'In fact, if I'd thought of all that before phoning the old boy, I would have spared him the visit.'

Jeanne smiled back at him. 'I doubt it,' she said. 'Well. Is there anything I can do?'

'That's a nice, polite question. And I know that the nice, polite answer is supposed to be, "Thank you, no."' His smile faded, and all at once Jeanne realised that there was a terrible weariness in his eyes. 'But, if the offer's genuine——'

'It is,' she said quickly. 'Just tell me how I can I help.'

'Well, Mrs Jacobs won't be back for an hour or two. But I thought Abby might agree to a cup of tea, if I brought it to her.'

'I'll make it, if you like.'

Gray gave her a grateful smile. 'Thanks. That'll give me the chance to change into jeans or something more comfortable than this.' Their eyes met, and he cleared his throat. 'I was—I was going to London, on business. But it can wait.'

Jeanne nodded. 'You go on, then. I'll make your aunt some tea. Do you think she might like some toast?'

Gray smiled. 'She might, if you brought it to her.'

'I'll put up some coffee, too—if you trust me to use the machine.'

His smile became a grin. 'Don't tell anyone in this house I said so, but this is the only place in the world where I've tasted burned coffee.'

'I could put up some bacon and eggs, too, if you like.'

'If I like?' He smiled. 'I'll be your slave forever, madam, if you do.'

She smiled, too. 'You don't have to go quite that far.'

Gray's laughter faded, and suddenly he was looking at her as he had last night, in the garden.

'Tell me how far you want me to go, then,' he said.

The air seemed suddenly charged with electricity. Their eyes met and held until, at last, Jeanne turned away and busied herself at the refrigerator.

'Breakfast in ten minutes,' she said briskly.

She waited until she heard Gray's footfalls exit the kitchen, and then she shut the refrigerator door and leaned her forehead against its cool surface.

I'll wait and tell him I'm going after breakfast, she thought. Yes. After breakfast. Definitely.

But the doctor arrived, just as they were having their second cups of coffee.

'Where's the old dragon?' he asked with a good-tempered smile, and Gray led the way to his aunt's rooms. Jeanne rinsed the dishes and loaded them into the dishwasher, then went into the library while she waited to hear the results of the doctor's examination.

She sprang to her feet when the two men entered the room. 'How is she?' she asked, looking from one face to the other.

The doctor smiled wryly. 'Abigail should take up the practice of medicine. She insisted she was fine and she is, all things considered. She just needs some rest. And her medication.'

Gray's eyes met Jeanne's. His lips twitched. 'I thought you might say that, John.'

Ethridge lowered his head and stared at Gray from under his bushy brows. 'You can't tell that woman a thing, you know. She's a tough old bird, your aunt.'

Gray and Jeanne smiled at each other. 'She asked if you'd come up and sit with her a while, Jeannie. Would you mind?'

'No, of course not. I'll be happy to.'

Jeanne started up the stairs while Gray showed Ethridge to the door. Outside Abigail's room, she paused, her hand on the doorknob.

She hadn't told Gray she was leaving. Well, there had been no chance, really. Besides, she couldn't go now, not while Abigail was ill.

Tomorrow, then. Or the day after. She nodded as she knocked, then opened the bedroom door. Yes. By the day after tomorrow, she'd certainly be on her way.

*   *   *

But the day after tomorrow came and went, and there was no possible way to tell either Gray or his aunt that she had decided to go back to the States.

'I don't know what I'd do without you, dear,' Abigail said one morning, as Jeanne brought her a cup of camomile tea.

Jeanne smiled and thanked her. 'But it isn't true, you know. I'm not doing anything special.'

'Oh, but you are,' Abigail answered. 'You're very special. Isn't she, Gray?'

'That isn't what I said,' she started to say, but Gray's words cut across hers.

'Yes,' he said quietly. 'She is.'

The days, and evenings became a peaceful blur. She spent mornings with Abigail, reading, chatting, sometimes just sitting beside the old woman as she dozed. After lunch, Gray escorted his aunt downstairs, to the garden, where she took the sun while Jeanne and Gray sat with her.

They dined at six so that Abigail could retire early—after much protest—and then Jeanne and Gray sat in the library, a fire burning in the hearth to chase the evening chill.

Jeanne thought she had never talked to anyone about so many things in her life. Gray had a hoard of funny stories about his days at university that could always make her laugh. And he seemed to know all the right people in London; his anecdotes about them were incisive and clever.

Not that they laughed over everything. Sometimes they argued. About the latest political scandal back home, the merits of cricket as opposed to baseball, whether heavy metal or country music was hardest on the ears.

Other times, they sat quietly reading. It was a pleasant, relaxed existence, a world apart from the way things had been between them before the party. They were at ease in a way they had never been. Sometimes, Jeanne almost wondered if she had dreamed what had happened that night in the garden—until one evening she looked up from her book and found Gray watching her.

She smiled at him, but he didn't respond. A curious lightness radiated through her body. He was looking at her so strangely—almost as if he had never seen her before.

'Gray? What is it?'

She thought, at first, that he hadn't heard her, but then he stirred in his chair.

'I was just thinking—this must be awfully dull for you. Spending your days as companion to an old lady, your evenings sitting quietly by the fire.'

Jeanne smiled and closed her book. 'Have I complained?'

He smiled in return. 'No. No, you haven't.'

'Well, then?'

'Still, this must be very different from the kind of life you're used to. Manhattan's all bright lights and noise. And you probably know dozens of people.' His smile tilted. 'I'll bet you're never home two evenings in a row.'

She sighed. 'I'm usually in bed and asleep by nine, if you want to know the truth.'

Gray's eyes fixed on her face. 'That's hard to imagine,' he said, his voice suddenly very quiet. 'A young, beautiful woman like you—why would the men in your life leave you a moment's solitude?'

'There aren't . . .' She fell silent. There aren't any men in my life, she'd almost said. But he wouldn't believe that, not considering the things he thought he knew about her. Tell him, she thought suddenly, tell him the truth.

But if she did, what would happen? Little sister, he'd called her in that deprecatingly sardonic way of his. He hadn't called her that in days, not since that night in the garden. Would he again, if he knew how inexperienced she really was?

It was a risk too great to run. She wasn't his sister; she didn't ever want to be. She wanted—she wanted . . .

'Aren't what?'

She looked up, pulled from her thoughts by the sudden intensity in his voice. Gray's eyes were dark, as dark as they had been that night beside the reflecting pool.

Jeanne drew a deep breath. 'There aren't any late nights, not if you've an early morning audition facing you.' He was still watching her with that same dark look. 'Especially—especially if it's a television audition,' she said nervously. 'The camera picks up everything. It shows——'

'It could only show how lovely you are,' he said, his voice gone thick. Silence fell over the room, and then Gray got quickly to his feet. 'Let's go somewhere.'

She looked at him, trying to control the sudden charge of excitement she felt.

'What about Abigail?'

'Nancy and Mrs Jacobs are both in the house. Anyway, Abby's her old self again; Ethridge gave her a clean bill of health today.' His hand closed over hers, and he drew her to her feet. 'I want to let the world see you on my arm,' he said softly. 'Do you mind?'

Her heart turned over. 'No,' she whispered. 'No, I don't mind at all.'

He took her to a little café tucked into the bank of the river, apologising in advance because he thought she might find it too quiet. But she loved the place on sight. Who wouldn't love the thick stone walls, low-beamed ceiling, and enormous hearth? she thought, gazing around as she sat opposite him in a small booth.

Gray had fed a handful of coins into the jukebox, and soft music played in the background.

'This is wonderful,' she said softly.

He smiled at her. 'It's not quite what I had in mind for our first date, but I'm glad you're pleased.'

Our first date. The simple words sent a rush of pleasure through her. He was right—this was, indeed, their first date. But how could that be, when she was—when she was in love with him?

The realisation made her breath catch. God, oh, God, she loved him. She loved him! Why had it taken her so long to admit it?

'Jeannie? Are you OK?'

She looked across the table at him. 'Gray,' she whispered. 'Gray...'

He smiled into her eyes. 'Let's dance,' he said softly.

She rose slowly, as if in a dream, and he led her to the tiny dance-floor and into his arms. It felt like coming home, she thought as she settled into his embrace. Sighing, she laid her head against his shoulder, and his arms tightened around her. His mouth brushed her temple, as light as the wing of a butterfly.

The music was slow, and they barely moved to it. When it finally ended, they stood in each other's arms for a moment, looking into each other's eyes, and then Gray smiled.

'Jeannie,' he said softly. He put his hand to her cheek, his thumb stroking across the curve of her jaw. 'Jeannie, I have to talk to you.'

Her pulse leaped. He loved her. That was what he wanted to tell her. He loved her, he...

'Let's get out of here.'

She waited while he tossed a handful of notes on the table and then, somehow, they were in his car, hurtling swiftly through the night before a vestige of sanity returned to her.

She had to tell him the truth about herself now, she thought, watching his shadowed profile. Would it please him to know of her innocence? Would it please him to know he was the only man she had ever wanted to give herself to?

The car turned down a dark lane and stopped beside a thick stand of trees. Gray turned to her; she could just make out his features.

'Jeannie. I should have told you this sooner. But...'

She leaned forward and laid her fingers lightly over his mouth. 'Gray—before you say anything, listen to me.'

'You don't owe me any explanations,' he said quickly, catching her wrist in his hand. I don't want——'

'But I do,' she said, her words cutting across his. 'You have to understand about me. About—about the men you think I—— '

'That's none of my business.' His tone was brusque. 'Your life——'

'Do you have any idea what it can be like to have someone else always watching over you?' she asked quickly.

'No. Not really. Well, my parents were pretty strict when I was a kid, but——'

'Mine were impossible. And it never changed, not even when I was grown up. Between them and Seth, I never got the chance to stand on my own two feet.'

Gray's hand fell away from her. 'I told you, you don't have to explain. You needed to break away, and you did.'

'I needed to breathe,' she said, her voice rising. 'I was choking. I was...' She drew a deep breath. 'Some-times—sometimes love can strangle you. Do you see?'

'No,' he said after a moment. 'I don't think I do. How can love do that?'

Jeanne sighed. 'I suppose it's hard for someone who's always been free to understand.'

'Free?' He laughed, and the sound of it surprised her by its harshness. 'Lord, you talk as if being loved were the same as being enslaved.'

'But it can be like that, when you want freedom.'

He grew still. 'I see,' he said softly.

Jeanne twisted towards him. 'Do you really?'

Gray nodded. 'Oh, yes,' he said, turning to stare out of the windscreen, 'I do, indeed. You came late to indepen-dence——'

'Yes,' she said eagerly. 'Exactly.'

'Which is why you made the most of it when you finally got it.'

She thought of the mess she'd almost made of her life over Charlie, the near-disaster of her marriage to George, and she laughed.

'No, Gray, I wouldn't say that. I haven't made the most of my independence. Not at all.'

His head swung towards her. 'I see,' he said in a silken whisper. 'There's more to come, then.'

She smiled shyly. 'Yes. At least, I hope so.'

His hands tightened on the steering-wheel. 'I don't suppose you'd care to be more specific?'

There was more to tell him, so much more, but she longed to be in his arms, even for a moment. Slowly, she lifted her hand and lay it on his arm.

'I think that's up to you,' she whispered.

She felt his bicep clench beneath her fingers. There was a silence, a long one, and then Gray's breath rasped in his throat.

'Yes,' he said, 'I suppose it is.'

There was a sudden coolness in his voice that she had not heard in a long, long time. He turned to her; she could see the white glint of his teeth in the darkness.

'You're about to get your cherished independence back,' he said. He moved his arm, and her hand fell away from him. 'That's what I wanted to tell you.' He smiled again as he reached to the ignition switch and turned the key. 'This evening's been by way of celebrating, you see.'

The engine roared to life, and the car moved forward. Jeanne stared at Gray's dark profile.

'What do you mean?'

His foot came down on the accelerator and the car skidded on to the narrow dirt road.

'Something's come up at my office.' He shifted, and the car leaped forward. 'I'm afraid I have to cut my holiday short. I'm returning to London in the morning.'

She stared at him. 'But——'

'Aren't I making myself clear? I'm heading back to the city tomorrow. You're to stay at Caldwell House until I've made the arrangements for your flight home.'

Jeanne fell back against the seat, stunned. Leaving. He was leaving—that was what he'd wanted to tell her, not that he loved her. He had used her services as long as he'd needed them, and now...

'I'll break the news to Abigail.' He glanced over at her, then back to the road. 'It's probably easiest if we say you have to get home for an audition. What do you think?'

Tears rose in her eyes. 'I think—I think...' She pressed the back of her hand to her mouth and turned towards him. 'Gray.' Her voice was a whisper. 'What—what happened?'

His hands tightened on the steering-wheel. 'I told you. Something came up in the city. I have to go to my office.'

'I meant—I meant, what happened just now? I thought, tonight, I thought...'

His head swung sharply towards her; in the reflected light of the dashboard, she could see the cruel line of his mouth.

'I know what you thought. And I did, too, for a while.' He looked back at the road, unwinding like a yellow ribbon in the glare of the car's headlights. 'But I like to make my own choices.'

She felt nausea rise in her throat. 'Your own choices?'

'Yeah. I pick the time, the place—and the woman.' A cold smile curved across his lips. 'It's the ultimate lesson you have to learn about being all grown up, Jeanne. Adults know when to say "no."'

Gray slammed his foot to the floor and the car raced forward into the night.

CHAPTER TEN

JEANNE stood at the lace curtains in her bedroom and stared at the garden through a translucent veil of grey rain.

The gloom of the morning suited her mood. Gray's words, spoken so coldly last night, still echoed in her mind.

'Adults know when to say "no".'

A sudden gust of wind-driven rain swept through the garden, ruffling the dark waters in the reflecting pool. Jeanne turned away, shuddering, as if the chill had somehow penetrated the glass.

At first it had seemed impossible to figure out what had happened. But suddenly realisation had come to her, so clearly that she'd wondered at her stupidity in not having anticipated it.

Last night had been an act of revenge. Graham Caldwell, whose ego was as enormous as his arrogance, had never forgiven her for the way she'd spurned his early advances—she had only to remember his behaviour each time she'd turned him aside to know that much. He'd bided his time, played on her emotions, waited until the moment she might surrender, then rejected her with a callousness so vicious it had left her shaken to the marrow of her bones.

That she had wanted to give herself to such a man, that she had thought herself in love with him, horrified her. In fact, Jeanne thought, as she walked slowly to the wardrobe, her behaviour since the day they'd met on that quiet road horrified her.

She had let Gray take over her life, that was what she had done. Oh, her reasons for staying on, for participating in his scheme, were her own. Angry at Seth, she'd let her own foolish pride trap her at Caldwell House.

But Gray didn't know that. He thought he'd been pulling the strings all along. And he still thought that, damn him! Jeanne's eyes narrowed as she remembered what had happened when they'd pulled into the driveway.

Gray had reached out as she started to open the car door, catching her by the wrist before she could escape.

'You're to make no explanations to my aunt. I'll take care of that in the morning, before I leave for London.'

Jeanne stared into his harsh, unforgiving face as he loomed over her.

'You're the one who's been lying to her all along. You damned well ought to be the one to——'

His grasp on her tightened. 'Spare me the moralising, Jeanne. It doesn't become you.'

'Bullying becomes you,' she said, her cool voice no reflection of the turmoil she felt. 'Take your hand off me.'

'Don't push me,' he warned softly.

Her heart skipped a beat. There was a controlled rage about him that terrified her. Somehow she managed to keep her eyes steady on his.

'Leave me alone!'

'For all time, and with the greatest of pleasure. Just as soon as I've made arrangements for your flight home.'

'I can make my own arrangements.'

He smiled coldly. 'Yes, I'm sure you can. But I've a responsibility to Seth. I promised him I'd take care of you while you were at Caldwell House.'

She felt something that was not quite laughter rise in her throat.

'Oh, that's marvellous! I wonder what my brother would say if he knew how his honourable old friend, Graham Caldwell, had exercised that responsib——'

The breath hissed in her throat as the sudden pressure of his hand on the fragile bones in her wrist forced her back against the seat.

'Stop now,' he whispered. 'Or you may end up regretting it.'

It had taken all her courage to meet his eyes. 'Take your hand off me,' she'd repeated, her voice steady.

Time had slowed while they'd stared at each other. He had seemed capable of almost anything at that moment, and, for the first time, Jeanne was afraid of him. At last, when she'd almost given up hope, his fingers had loosened, then fallen away from her. He'd swung away, leaned back in his seat and wrapped his hands tightly around the steering-wheel, his knuckles white against the dark wood.

'Go on,' he'd said, 'get out.'

Jeanne had scrambled from the car, no longer caring what he might think of her haste as she made good her escape.

Now, remembering, her hands balled into fists. What kind of fool was she, for God's sake? Here she was, hours later, acting the role of docile prisoner, waiting for Gray to make arrangements for her return to the States as if she were, indeed, the child he'd accused her of being.

She gritted her teeth and threw open the wardrobe door. Doing what he'd told her to do was nonsense. He had left for London hours ago—she'd heard the roar of his car as he drove off.

There was nothing to stop her from taking command of her own life again.

'You can stuff your orders,' Jeanne said aloud as she began yanking her things from the wardrobe and tossing them on the bed.

She'd got to Warwickshire on her own, and that was how she'd leave it. And to hell with Graham Caldwell.

The hard part was saying goodbye to Abigail, even though the old woman was gracious about the sudden disruption in her household. She nodded her understanding, then patted the couch cushion beside her.

'It's all right, dear,' she said as Jeanne sank on to the couch. 'Graham explained that you've both been called away. I understand.'

'I hope so,' Jeanne said uneasily. 'I feel badly leaving you alone.'

Abigail smiled. 'Hardly alone. Nancy's here, and Mrs Jacobs. And I've finally let Graham convince me that the Barstow girl—she has a nursing degree, and she plays awfully good bridge—would be a fine companion. She'll be here later this morning.' Her pale hands clasped in her lap and she looked up at Jeanne. 'I must admit, I had hoped things would work out differently.'

'I'm sure you did.' Jeanne hesitated. 'But it wasn't— I mean, your nephew and I never...'

'It's all right, dear.' Abigail smiled reassuringly. 'I understand. These things don't always end as we'd wished.'

Guilt weighed on Jeanne's shoulders like a yoke. 'I wish I could explain.'

'Jeanne.' Abigail put her hand under Jeanne's chin and lifted it. 'I'm going to let you in on a little secret.' She paused dramatically. 'I know all about Graham's little ruse.'

Jeanne stared at her. 'All about...?'

'Of course. It was dreadfully transparent. You children snapped at each other almost as much as you smiled— but even that gave me hope. What is it they say about love and hate being two sides of the same coin?'

'Well, there was only one side to Gray and me,' Jeanne said softly. 'I'm just sorry we deceived you.'

The old woman cocked her head. 'I wonder if perhaps it isn't yourselves you've deceived.'

'How?'

Abigail sighed. 'I told you, I'm just an old romantic. But I think you and my nephew really care about each other.'

'No,' Jeanne said quickly. 'No, we don't.'

The pale blue eyes turned piercing as they fixed on Jeanne's face.

'Is that what you want to believe—or what you really believe?'

Jeanne swallowed drily. 'Perhaps—perhaps, for a little while, I thought—I may have let myself hope...' She fell silent. The women's eyes met, held, and then Jeanne looked away. 'I don't want to talk about it,' she whispered. 'I'm sorry.'

Abigail patted her hand. 'Is there anything I can do?'

'No. No, thank you. I've called for a taxi—it should be here any minute.'

The old woman frowned. 'I still think you should wait for Graham's call. He said he'd phone as soon as he'd arranged for your ticket.'

Jeanne shook her head. 'I'll be fine.'

'Will you? Have you enough money?'

'Yes, more than enough. My replacement traveller's cheques came through the other day.'

'And what about a hotel room in London? It's the height of the season, dear. Rooms are hard to come by.'

Jeanne smiled reassuringly. 'I telephoned Claverley House—the place I stayed at before I—before I came here.'

Abigail nodded. 'Well, then, I suppose it'll be all right.'

A horn sounded in the driveway. 'That'll be my taxi,' Jeanne said. A lump rose in her throat as she looked at Abigail, and then she gave her a quick hug. 'Goodbye,' she said. 'And don't worry about me—I'll be OK.'

She was—until she reached Claverley House. It was still raining, but the train trip to the city had been pleasant, the taxi ride from Euston Station to the hotel swift. But Jeanne's plans began to come undone as she stood at the reception desk, facing Claverley House's pleasant, but implacable, manager.

'I am sorry, Miss Lester. But we've no reservation in your name. If you could just tell me who it was you spoke with?'

'How do I know? Whoever answers your phone, that's who. And he said——'

'Yes, yes, so you say. But we've no room booked for you, and none available.'

Her shoulders slumped. They had gone around this way twice already; she knew there was no point in doing it again.

'All right, then, I'd appreciate it if you'd phone another hotel on my behalf.'

'I wish I could. But I tried booking rooms elsewhere for a gentleman only minutes ago. I'm afraid there's nothing, Miss Lester. There are several conventions in the city, you see, and it's mid-summer.'

Jeanne glared at the man. 'Look, I'm trying to be reasonable about this. But you can't just throw up your hands and ignore me. What am I supposed to do? Sleep in the street?'

'It would serve you bloody well right,' a furious male voice said.

Her heart lurched. She swung around and found herself staring into the glowering face of Graham Caldwell.

'What are you doing here?' she demanded.

'Bailing you out again,' he said grimly, 'a function which is growing increasingly tiresome. Is that your suitcase?'

He seemed to take her silence as an answer. She watched as he lifted the case and, without a backward glance, strode across the reception area to the door.

'Wait a minute,' she called, trotting after him. 'Just what do you think you're doing?'

He paused and gave her a smile that glittered with malice. 'Taking you to a room for the night, *darling*. Isn't that what you said you wanted?'

Heads turned. Jeanne felt her cheeks flame. His eyes were cold, the warning light smouldering in their dark blue depths. Don't provoke me, he was saying, not unless you want the game to escalate.

There was nothing to do but grit her teeth and follow him on to the pavement.

'All right,' she said, once they were clear of the door and standing under the canopy, 'that's enough. I don't know how you found me, but——'

'You told Abby where you were going, and she told me. My car's parked just over there.'

'I don't care where your car's parked,' she said angrily. 'I am not going anywhere with you. If you think you can just walk in and—and——'

'Don't make a scene.' His voice was chill.

'I am not making a...' Jeanne glanced up. The doorman was watching them, a smile of amusement on his face. 'I'm not making a scene,' she said more quietly. 'But I demand to know by what right you think you can come along and strong-arm me.'

Gray opened the boot of his car, tossed in her luggage, then opened the passenger door.

'Get in.'

'I will not.'

A muscle moved in his jaw. 'Get in,' he said softly. 'Or I'll load you in with as much ceremony as I did your suitcase.'

She stared at him. He was as taut as a drawn bow. She said something under her breath, then did as he'd ordered. Gray slammed the door after her, then went quickly around to the driver's side.

'I am not going back to Warwickshire,' she said as the car slipped into the London traffic. 'If you want to take me to the airport, that's fine. Otherwise...'

'Your flight to New York leaves in the morning.' He shoved an envelope at her. 'Here's your ticket.'

Jeanne nodded. 'Good. Then if you'd please take me to another hotel——'

Gray looked over at her, his face rigid with distaste. 'Why don't you do us both a favour and keep quiet?'

Jeanne's mouth trembled. To think she'd ever dreamed she felt anything for this man.

'With pleasure,' she said, and then she clamped her lips together and stared fixedly out of the window into the sombre grey of a rainy London afternoon.

The car drew up in front of a narrow, three-storey building on a quiet cul-de-sac. Out of the corner of her eye, Jeanne could see Gray unbuckling his seatbelt, and she ached to ask him where they were and why they'd stopped. But even that seemed too much conversation to offer to this silent, stone-faced man, and so she bit her lip and swallowed her questions.

His door opened, then slammed shut.

'Let's go,' he said impatiently, coming around to her side of the car and pulling open the door.

'What for? Why have we——'

'This is where you'll spend the night. Tomorrow morning, a taxi will take you to Heathrow.'

Jeanne looked at the narrow building warily. It was made of red brick, with geranium-filled window-boxes, and it was rather handsome-looking. The cul-de-sac itself was quiet.

'Is this a hotel? I don't see a sign.'

Gray grasped her elbow. 'Come on,' he said impatiently. 'It's wet out here.'

'I'm not moving until I know where we are. You said you'd take me to a hotel.'

'There are no hotel rooms. Didn't you hear what the manager said?'

'There must be somewhere,' she said stubbornly.

'There's a room here which will do just fine.'

She peered past him. 'What is this? A bed and breakfast?'

Gray smiled tightly. 'That's as good a description as any.' His hand tightened on her arm. 'Now, get out.'

Jeanne looked at him. His face was dark, his eyes cold and flat. Accommodating him in any fashion was a hateful idea. But if he had found her a room for the night, it would be foolish to turn it down. She nodded, then stepped out of the car.

'Very well. I can see myself in.'

He laughed aloud. 'No, you cannot.'

Gray took her arm and marched her to the front door. Her brows rose when he pulled a key from his pocket and inserted it into the lock.

'Don't you have to ring the——' The door swung open, and suddenly what was happening fell into place. 'Wait a minute,' she said quickly. 'Dammit, Graham Caldwell, you just wait a——'

Gray put his hand in the small of her back and gave her a shove. She stumbled into a small entry hall, gloomy and dark on this rain-swept afternoon. The door swung shut after them.

'All right,' he said grimly, 'now you can make the scene you were working up to.' He strode past her and flicked on the lights. '*Without* giving the neighbours a treat.'

Jeanne stared at him as he flipped the key into the air, then caught it in his hand and pocketed it.

'This isn't a bed and breakfast,' she said.

He smiled coldly and inclined his head. 'Give the young lady a round of applause.'

'It's—it's your home, isn't it?'

'Very good,' he said, shrugging off his suit jacket. 'You're bright enough when you put your mind to it.'

Jeanne whirled towards the door. 'I am not staying here. How dare you think you could——?'

His hands clamped on her shoulders and he spun her towards him.

'You'll stay.' His head lowered towards hers. 'You'll stay, if I have to carry you to your room and lock you in. I told you, you're my responsibility and you will be until the moment your plane lifts off.'

She had never felt so powerless in her life. Seth's well-meaning big brothering, her parents' loving meddling, all faded beside Gray Caldwell's arrogant domination.

'I hate you,' she whispered, lifting her chin and staring into his eyes. 'Do you hear me, Gray? I hate you!'

His eyes darkened, until they were the shade of the midnight sky. There was a coldness to him that terrified her; Jeanne was suddenly as frightened as she had been that long-ago night when she'd awakened to find him in her bed.

'I'll just bet you do,' he said in a growling whisper. 'It's not quite the sort of evening you'd planned for your last night in London, is it?'

'No,' she said, forcing a bravado she didn't feel, 'no, it isn't. And you've no right——'

'I don't give a damn about your "rights".' His grasp on her tightened. 'Seth is my friend, Jeanne. I know it's probably difficult for someone like you to understand, but I've a responsibility to him.'

'Isn't it a little late to think about that?' Her eyes met his in defiance. 'When you've been trying to seduce his sister?'

He gave her a smile so swift and chill that it made her heartbeat stutter.

'Is that what you call what was happening?' She cried out as his hands bit deep into her flesh. 'I think even Seth would agree I behaved like any other man. It was only in turning you down that I was different.'

Tears of rage glittered in her eyes. 'You bastard. You—you...'

Gray spun her towards the stairs and put his hand in the small of her back.

'I'm sure you'll figure out what to call me by tomorrow morning. But I'd prefer you work on your vocabulary in private.'

He showed her to a small, pleasant room on the second floor. 'The bath's through that door,' he said, as tonelessly as an innkeeper. 'Dinner's at seven. Please be prompt.'

'Why? So you can lock me back in my cage before the sun sets?'

He turned to her, his hand on the doorknob. 'Remember what I said last night, Jeanne?' His voice was soft as velvet. 'Don't push.'

Her chin lifted. 'You don't scare me,' she said.

But she'd hesitated just long enough so the door had safely closed between them before she spoke. She stared at it, then flung her handbag at the wall. It slid harmlessly to the carpet, and after a moment Jeanne slid, equally harmlessly, to the edge of the narrow bed and sank down on it.

'I really do hate you, Graham Caldwell,' she whispered.

The tears that had threatened came then, tears she told herself were surely of anger and confusion more than anything else. Jeanne lay back on the bed. After a while, lulled by the sound of the rain, exhausted by her own turbulent emotions, she slept. And, slowly, she fell into a dream.

She dreamed that the rain had changed to snow, a gentle fall that covered the green English meadows in a blanket of white. She was walking slowly along a narrow country lane. Behind her, the strains of Lohengrin drifted on the breeze.

She glanced down at herself. She was dressed in white lace, she realised with surprise, a bell-skirted gown that went to the ground, with a long train stretching gracefully behind.

It was a wedding gown. But why? She wasn't marrying George; that was all done with. Besides, this was not the gown she'd worn that afternoon. Hers had been simple and sensible, the kind that suited a simple, sensible union.

Her heart thudded as a man stepped out of the trees. His face was in shadow, but she knew who he was. He had a way of holding himself that said he would always get what he wanted.

She whispered his name, half afraid that if she said it too loudly, he would vanish. Her steps quickened, and suddenly the shadow lifted and she could see his face.

It was Gray. Gray, smiling as he started towards her; Gray, holding out his arms to embrace her; Gray...

His image shimmered, became wraithlike. 'No,' she said, 'no. Gray, don't leave me. Wait. Please.'

Jeanne began to run. Her breathing grew laboured, her legs began to ache—but the dreamlike landscape never changed. She was running as hard as she could, but she was gaining no ground. And Gray was fading, fading, she would never reach him in time. She would be lost in this dream forever.

'Wait,' she cried. 'Please. Please, don't leave me. I beg you. Don't. Gray, please.'

'Don't cry, Jeannie.'

Strong arms closed around her. Jeanne sobbed and burrowed into the hard warmth of a welcome embrace.

'I don't want it to end like this,' she whispered. 'Not like this.'

'You're right,' a deep voice murmured. 'It shouldn't end like this. And it won't.'

She sighed, secure in the strength and comfort of those arms. There was a strong, steady heartbeat beneath her ear, a clean, masculine scent in her nostrils...

Jeanne's eyes flew open and she stared into the face of Graham Caldwell.

'Easy,' he said as she started to struggle. 'Easy, Jeannie. You're all right now.'

She swallowed hard. 'What happened?'

'You were having a bad dream.'

Her eyes fell shut as she remembered, not just the dream but the panic that had accompanied it—the panic that came of knowing she had lost Gray forever.

'Yes,' she whispered. 'I—I must have dozed off, and—and...'

'Jeannie.' Gray clasped her chin and lifted her face from his shoulder. 'Look at me.'

She didn't want to. God only knew what Gray would be able to read in her tear-streaked face. But the gentle pressure of his hand persisted, and finally she raised her damp lashes.

The rage she had seen in his face ever since last night was gone. In its place was something indefinable—something bitter-sweet, that brought a lump to her throat.

'I was wrong, Jeannie. I've no right to lock you up here.' He stroked damp tendrils of chestnut hair from her flushed cheeks. 'You were right about something else, too. Our time together shouldn't end this way.' He hesitated. 'You and I—you and I have had a very special holiday together.' He smiled. 'Don't you agree?'

A very special holiday. Gray, she thought, Gray...

'I think we should declare a truce.' He clasped her shoulders and put her gently from him. 'In fact, what we ought to do is make the most of our last evening together.'

Jeanne stared at him. 'I don't understand,' she whispered.

Gray smiled at her. 'How would you like to see the real London, the one visitors rarely glimpse?'

She was almost afraid to answer for fear of breaking the spell. 'Do you mean—do you mean, with you?'

'We'll dine at the Connaught and dance at a place in Soho. How does that sound?'

Like a night in paradise, she thought, but not because of the places he would take her. She would be with Gray, with the man she loved—and how could she ever have tried to tell herself she didn't?

But she was not fool enough to say that to him. Not yet—although who knew what miracles the night would bring?

Jeanne smiled. 'It sounds wonderful,' she said softly.

Months later, she would remember her own naïveté and weep.

CHAPTER ELEVEN

JEANNE had seen the Connaught, one of London's most elegant hotels, from the outside during her brief stay in the city weeks before. She had longed to enter the handsome old building, but she had found its legendary reputation intimidating. Small, old-fashioned, the Connaught never advertised, yet turned away more guests than it accepted.

She felt a flush of pleasure as Gray led her into the wood-panelled lobby. Oriental rugs, as rich in colour and design as any she'd ever imagined, stretched across dark wood floors. A staircase rose ahead, its banisters old and polished to a deep lustre.

'Would you like a drink before dinner?' Gray asked.

Jeanne looked at him and nodded, eyes shining. 'If you like.'

He smiled and put his hand across hers as it lay on his arm. 'You'll like the bar—it reminds me of Abigail's parlour.'

He was right. The bar was actually a series of small, wood-panelled rooms, furnished with upholstered chairs and fine wood tables that could easily have come from Caldwell House.

'What would you like?' Gray asked, and Jeanne looked at him and shook her head.

'I don't know,' she said, and she laughed softly. 'I usually order a glass of white wine, but I've the feeling that's far too pedestrian a request in a place like this.'

He smiled, then looked up at the waiter hovering discreetly beside them. 'We'll have a bottle of Dom Perignon '79.'

The man inclined his head, then hurried off. Jeanne sighed, then settled back in her chair.

'This is lovely,' she said. 'Thank you for bringing me.'

'Thank you for coming.' Gray's eyes sought hers. 'You can't imagine how often I've pictured us sitting here, beside the fire, just this way.'

She looked at him in surprise. He was watching her with a steadiness that made her breath quicken.

'Have you?' she asked softly.

Gray nodded. 'I almost suggested we drive down to London last weekend.'

'Did you?'

He nodded again. 'Yes.' His voice was low and a little rough; the sound of it sent a tremor along her skin. 'I thought—I hoped...'

'What did you hope?' Jeanne whispered.

But their waiter appeared with their champagne and the dinner menus before Gray could answer. By the time the wine had been opened and poured and their meal planned, both of them had retreated from unanswerable questions. And so they talked of inconsequential things, of the latest films and books.

'You mean, you've actually read C.S. Forester?' Gray asked in amazement.

Jeanne grinned. 'Why do you look so shocked? When I was little, I read all the things girls are supposed to read. Nancy Drew, Judy Blume...'

'Who are they? And how could they have led you to C.S. Forester and a character like Horatio Hornblower?'

'Hornblower? Who's Hornblower? I'm talking about Rosie Sayers in *The African Queen*.'

Gray laughed. 'Ah, yes, Rosie. Well, she and Charlie Allnutt were fine, but they can't hold a candle to Lady Barbara and the good captain.' He leaned back and shook his head. 'So, you're telling me that the image I have of a shiny-faced moppet in a frilly dress, surrounded by dolls and teddy bears, is all wrong.'

Jeanne smiled. 'No, not entirely. I loved dolls and teddies and all that goes with them.' Her smile dimmed a little. 'It's just that as I got older, I began longing to try something different. It's hard to explain.'

'You told me how protective your family was of you. So you lived your adventures through the books you read. That's not so strange; lots of people do.'

'Yes,' she said, surprised and touched by his quick understanding. 'Yes, exactly.' She smiled. 'Books—and dreams. My mother used to tease me sometimes; she'd say if I wasn't careful, I'd get lost in a dream.'

His eyes darkened and fastened on hers. 'Do you still dream, Jeannie?'

The sudden softness in his voice was like a caress. 'Yes,' she murmured, colour rising under her skin as she remembered the dream she had had only hours before. 'Sometimes I do.'

His hand reached for hers and clasped it lightly. 'What do you dream of now?' he asked quietly.

She swallowed, afraid to answer. Gray's fingers tightened on hers. They sat staring at each other. Suddenly there was the discreet sound of a throat being cleared.

'Your table is ready, sir.'

Gray's mouth twisted. 'Thank you.' He rose and offered Jeanne his arm.

They dined in a beautiful cream-coloured room beneath crystal chandeliers. Their banquette was spacious and private, the food delicious, from Scotch salmon and caviare to Dover sole and asparagus to sugar-glazed grapes and perfect strawberries dipped in chocolate.

But, Jeanne thought, as she stole a glance at Gray from beneath her lashes, they could have been eating at McDonald's, munching on hamburgers and fries, and it still would have been as wonderful.

She was happy, happier than she had ever been, and it had nothing to do with the perfect meal or the elegant surroundings.

She was happy because she was with Gray.

'What are you thinking?'

She looked up, startled. He was watching her as he had been earlier, his eyes dark with intensity.

'I—I . . .' She looked at him helplessly. 'Nothing,' she said finally. 'I mean, I was thinking how lovely all this is.'

'You're what's lovely, Jeannie.' Gray's eyes swept over her. 'I like your hair that way.'

Her hand went quickly to the shining chestnut mass. She had brushed it back from her face and pinned it loosely on the top of her head. A few stray strands had escaped; she felt them brush against her fingers. She felt suddenly shy and nervously began to tuck them up.

'Don't,' he said quickly. Their eyes met. 'It looks— it looks as if it's coming undone, as if you'd started taking the pins down just for me.'

A rush of heat sped through her blood. They stared at each other, and just when Jeanne felt as if she were going to explode, Gray tossed his napkin on the table and signalled for their waiter.

'I've made reservations at Daffy's,' he said. 'We don't want to be late.'

She blinked, surprised at his matter-of-fact tone. His expression was inscrutable; she wondered if she'd imagined what had happened only seconds ago.

'Have you heard of it?' He smiled politely as he scrawled his name to the dinner bill. 'It's London's newest club. I think you'll enjoy it.'

And she might have, under other circumstances. Daffy's gleamed with chrome and black patent furnishings. The walls were mirrored, the dance-floor transparent vinyl laid over brightly flashing lights, and the clientele looked as if it had been plucked from the pages of *People* magazine.

It would have been an exciting place to visit, if she'd been with George or Charlie or any one of half a dozen other men. But tonight she was with Gray, which meant that the music was too loud, the lights too bright, the decibel-level too high. And the aura of frenetic gaiety only seemed to emphasise the sudden silence that had fallen over them.

'Would you like to dance?'

Jeanne looked up. Gray was watching her, his eyes hooded, his lips in a smile that seemed drawn on his face. She glanced at the dance-floor, where couples were gyrating to an old Rolling Stones hit. No, she thought, she didn't want to dance—not like that. What she wanted were soft lights and violins; slow, dreamy music, and a dance-floor so small and crowded that Gray would have no choice but to take her in his arms and hold her close.

But instinct warned her that sitting here was not a good idea, either. Gray was as uncomfortable as she, but why? Everything had been fine, better than fine, until . . .

'Jeanne?' She looked up and he smiled and held out his hand. 'Come on. Let's give it a try.'

He led her to the lighted floor. She fell in opposite him and they began to move with the music. She felt stiff at first, but Gray was a good dancer, relaxed and at ease, and after a while she felt the heavy beat of the music begin to throb deep within her bones.

'Having fun?'

She nodded and smiled at him. It was easier than trying to make herself heard over the pounding music. She *was* having fun, even though she hadn't expected to. Gray was enjoying himself, too. Suddenly, she was very glad he had brought her here. Maybe the good-natured crowd and the flashing lights could help restore the happiness that had seemed just within their grasp at dinner.

The floor grew crowded; bodies jostled against bodies. Gray grinned and began to dance faster. Jeanne tossed her head and laughed. She had some moves he hadn't even imagined.

She shimmied her hips, then dropped back a step just as the dancer behind her did the same thing.

'Watch it!' Gray caught her in his arms before she could fall. He laughed down into her flushed face. 'Fancy footwork will only get you into trouble on a floor this jammed.'

'You're right,' she said, laughing with him.

Another couple whirled by, and Gray pulled her closer to him. 'It's dangerous out here. You could get hurt.'

She fell silent, watching as his smile dimmed, then fled. He was holding her tightly, his hands on her hips, almost cupping her bottom. Her breasts were pressed to his chest. She could feel the race of his heart, smell the scent of his body.

The crowd moved around them, leaving them alone in a tiny bubble of space and time. They stared into each other's eyes, and then Gray let go of her and stepped back.

'It's getting late,' he said. 'Maybe we ought to call it a night.'

Jeanne swallowed drily. 'Yes. You're probably right.'

'You'll want to get a good night's sleep. You've a long flight ahead of you tomorrow.'

'Thank you for reminding me,' she said with a polite little smile. 'I'd almost forgotten.'

Gray's eyes darkened. 'Yes,' he said, 'I had, too.'

The trip back to his house seemed to take forever. It had been such a lovely evening, until that moment on the dance-floor, when the passion that had always been between them had sprung to life again.

Gray had wanted her, despite what he thought of her.

She shifted in her seat and stared at him. What if she told him the truth? That she'd never even known what wanting a man was until she'd met him?

Her head fell back and she shut her eyes. What a stupid idea! He wouldn't believe her. And, even if he did, so what?

All she'd end up doing was embarrassing herself.

Tomorrow morning, Gray would put her on a plane and send her home, and then he'd go back to a life where there wasn't any room, wasn't any need, for a special woman—certainly not for her.

How long would it take before her face was nothing but a blur? Before he'd have difficulty remembering her name? But she—she would remember. She would remember and she would ache.

'Jeannie.'

Her eyes flew open. The car was pulled up before the house. Gray was leaning over her, smiling.

'I—I must have fallen asleep,' she said quickly. 'Sorry.'

He shook his head. 'For what?' His hand brushed lightly over her cheek. 'I hated to wake you—you looked so peaceful.'

'Gray?'

His breath whispered against her face. 'What?'

She stared at him. I love you, she thought, Gray, I love you so much...

'I—I just wanted to tell you how lovely tonight was. Thank you.'

He looked at her for a long moment, and then he drew back. 'It's late.' His voice was brusque; he turned away and opened his door. She did the same, and they walked through the quiet cul-de-sac to the house.

At three in the morning, Jeanne pushed off the bed-covers and gave up her useless attempts at sleep. She had been lying there for almost two hours, watching as the hand of the clock moved slowly around the lighted dial, but all that had happened was that she grew more and more awake.

Maybe some warm milk would help. Gray had urged her to make herself feel at home, when they'd come in. He'd been almost painfully polite, going on and on about extra towels and fresh soap and morning coffee as they'd stood in the entry hall, and then, finally, a thick silence had fallen between them. Their eyes had met, and he'd turned away.

'Goodnight, Jeannie,' he'd said. 'I'm going to stay downstairs and read for a while.'

'Goodnight,' she'd said softly, and then she'd made her way slowly up the stairs.

Now, standing on the landing in the middle-of-the-night silence, Jeanne sighed and drew her silk robe closely around her. Gray's door was closed. At least one of them was sleeping, she thought, and she made her way quietly down the stairs to the kitchen.

The swinging door creaked as she pushed it open. The window blinds were partly open; light from the street lamp just outside the house drifted into the dark room.

She padded to the refrigerator and took out the milk. There had to be a saucepan somewhere, and a mug...

'Jeannie?'

Startled, she whirled towards the door. A shadowy figure stepped forward, and she let out her breath.

'Gray! Good lord, you scared the life out of me.' He stepped into the kitchen and she smiled apologetically. 'Did I wake you? I tried to be quiet, but...'

'I was in the library. What are you doing up?'

She turned away. 'I—I couldn't sleep. I thought I'd have some warm milk—if you don't mind.'

'No, of course not. Shall I put the light...?'

'No,' she said quickly. 'No, please don't. Would you like me to heat some milk for you, too?'

Gray hesitated, and then he laughed softly. 'Sure. Why not?'

She heard the squeal of a chair as he pulled it from the table and sat. There was a saucepan on the stove; she filled it with milk, then set it on the burner.

Gray cleared his throat. 'I guess you must be eager to get home,' he said.

'Yes,' she said quickly. Too quickly. Her hand shook as she took a pair of mugs from the shelf over the sink. 'I—I'm looking forward to it.'

She handed him a mug, then sat down across the table from him. Light from the street lamp just outside drifted through the half-closed blinds, softly illuminating him. Gray's hair was tousled; he was wearing a towelling robe, open to the waist. She could see his chest beneath it, and the dark mat of hair that curled across it.

A shudder went through her, and she drew her silk robe closer around her.

'Cold?'

'No,' she said quickly. 'I—I . . .' She stared across the table. He was watching her; his face was in shadow, but she could feel the intensity of his eyes on her.

Suddenly, she pushed back her chair and rose quickly to her feet. 'I think I'll take my milk to my room, if you don't——'

'Jeannie.' He rose, too. 'Jeannie, wait.'

Her heart thudded. 'Gray, please. I—I——'

He came around the table quickly. 'Do you know why I couldn't sleep?' His voice was thick, the words almost slurred. He reached out and clasped her shoulders. 'Because I couldn't stop thinking about you, lying asleep in a room just across from mine.'

Her head tilted back and she looked up at him. It was hard to see his features; harder still to see his eyes. But there was no mistaking his message. He wanted her; she knew that. She had always known it.

But there had been so many times he could have taken her. That first night, at the B and B when he'd been in her bed. They'd both known that; her struggles would have become whimpers of pleasure if he had persisted.

And the other night, when he'd taken her to the café in Warwickshire—she'd have let him make love to her then, but he'd turned her away with a cruelty that had almost destroyed her.

Then—then why now? Why tonight, when she was leaving in the morning?

'I'll never see you again after tomorrow,' Gray whispered, as if he had read her mind. His hands slid down her arms, to her waist. 'We'll both go our separate ways. And I'll wonder, for the rest of my life, what it would have been like to have made love to you, Jeannie.'

He bent and kissed her gently, the pressure of his lips on hers like the touch of a falling leaf. His hands slid up her ribs, and she caught her breath as they paused just under her breasts.

'Jeannie.' His breath warmed her cheek, and then her throat as he nipped lightly at the curving juncture of neck and shoulder. 'Let's not waste this night as we've wasted all the others.'

There were so many reasons to stop him. Jeanne's head spun.

If Gray made love to her, he would realise that she had lied to him all along. How would she explain? How would she survive their parting when her soul would be bound to his forever? He would never be hers; hadn't he just reminded her of that?

Gray had said that adults knew when to say 'no.' But that meant they also knew when to say 'yes,' she thought as his mouth took hers in a sweet, deep kiss. *She* would choose the moment, *she* would choose the time, *she* would choose the man—and Gray was that man. This choice, this moment, was hers and hers alone. And she would gather it to her heart and cherish it for years to come.

She felt the floor tilt beneath her feet. His hands were on her breasts, cupping them as her flesh swelled against his palms. And his body was moving against hers, the hardness of his arousal pulsing against her loins.

His need electrified her. She closed her eyes as he swung her up into his arms and carried her up the stairs and to his room. She could hear the race of his heart under her ear, its hammering as wild as hers.

He lowered her to her feet, then slowly undid the sash of her robe and drew it off. It slipped to the floor, and seconds later her nightgown fell on top of it in a silken cocoon.

Gray whispered her name as he ran his hand slowly over her body, his fingers sending shivers of heat from her throat to her thighs, and then he undid his robe and shrugged free of it.

She caught her breath as the moonlight washed over his naked body. His shoulders were broad, as was his chest. The dark mat of hair she had glimpsed tapered as it reached his navel. Her gaze swept lower. His body was hard, unashamedly aroused, and she felt herself flower at the sight of him.

'Jeannie.' He clasped her face in his hands and looked into her eyes. 'Tell me you want me.'

A tremor went through her. 'I've always wanted you, Gray. Always.'

He lowered her gently to the bed and then knelt beside her. 'So lovely,' he said softly. 'I knew you'd look like this—your skin like buttered honey, your breasts so perfect.' He bent and kissed her throat, then her breasts, and she cried out as he drew her nipple into the heat of his mouth. 'Touch me,' he whispered.

Her hands trembled as she reached to his broad shoulders. Her fingers skimmed down his muscled arms, to his chest, to his ridged abdomen. Gray caught her hands and brought them to his lips, lightly biting the soft flesh at the base of her thumbs, and then he took her in his arms and kissed her again and again, each kiss more demanding, more intense, than the last.

Waves of sensation flowed through her. Suddenly, something wild and fierce broke free within her. She reached between their damp bodies, her hand curling lightly around his heated flesh, and he cried out her name and rose above her.

'Now,' she heard herself whisper. 'Oh, now, Gray. Please.'

She was blind with desire and need, her body arcing towards his. Gray moaned, and suddenly he was inside her, thrusting, thrusting...

Her cry stopped him. Muscles rigid, his body froze above hers. 'Jeannie,' he whispered. 'My God, Jeannie! Why didn't you tell me? Why?'

He couldn't stop now. Not when she was almost his. Not when her heart and body were crying out for fulfilment.

Her plea was wordless, an urgent movement of her hips, but it was enough.

'My Jeannie,' he said and, even in the heated passion of their desire, she wondered at the catch in his voice.

But then he moved, penetrating her, and suddenly there was no time to wonder or to think, there was only Gray and the night and the fierce joy blossoming within her.

She cried out his name, and then she felt herself spin away into the darkness.

She awoke later, safe in Gray's arms. His breath sighed against her cheek.

'Why did you let me think you'd been with other men?' he asked softly.

The answers were as complex, and as simple, as the reason the sun rose in the sky each morning.

Because he'd stirred emotions so new they terrified her.

Because she'd fallen in love with him long before she was ready to admit the truth to herself.

But those were not the answers he wanted to hear.

'It's not something you just drop into a conversation,' she said as lightly as she could manage.

His hand traced a fiery path from her breast to her belly. 'Yes, but you let me think——'

'Does it matter?' Jeanne put her fingers lightly against his lips. The bed shifted under his weight and his hand fell away from her.

'Yes. It matters.' His voice had gone flat. Jeanne turned towards him. He had rolled to his back; he lay staring up at the ceiling, his arms folded beneath his head. 'All that stuff about being independent, about living your own life—what was all that about?'

Her heart lurched against her ribs. 'What do you mean?'

'What the hell do you think it means?' he said sharply. He turned towards her and rose up on his elbow. 'Exactly what happens now that you've given me your virginity?'

The little smile of happiness that had been on her lips trembled. Gray was already regretting what had happened. Not that she could blame him. A sexual encounter with an experienced woman was one thing. But taking your friend's sister's virginity was quite another.

'Nothing happens,' she said quickly.

'I see.' His hand moved, cupped her breast with an almost impersonal detachment. 'So what was I, then? Your initiation into the mysteries of womanhood?'

Jeanne swallowed again. 'That's—that's a crude way to put it, don't you think? But—but yes, I guess that sums it up. Of course, I'll always remember that you were my first lover.'

Gray rolled her beneath him. 'Hell,' he said in a harsh whisper, 'then I damned well better make this night one you won't forget.'

He took her then, with a swiftness that made her cry out and cling to him.

This night in Gray's arms was all she would have to remember for the rest of her life. Tears rose to her eyes, fell to her lips, and mingled in their kisses like warm rain.

I love you, she thought. And then she gave herself up to the dark whirlwind of their passion

At dawn, as a milky fog curled through the cobbled streets, Jeanne rose quietly, dressed, and slipped from the bedroom. She took her suitcase from her room, then tiptoed down the stairs and out of the door.

A street later, she found a taxi waiting at a stand.

'Heathrow,' she said to the driver as she climbed in. 'And hurry, please.'

'I'll do the best I can, ma'am, in this weather.'

Jeanne nodded. That was all anyone could do, she thought as the taxi tunnelled into the mist. It was what she had done, too.

It was easier to leave now, while Gray slept. This way, neither of them would have to face the embarrassment daylight would bring.

Her head fell back against the seat and she closed her eyes to the dreary morning as the taxi rolled on, carrying her further and further from the only man she would ever love—and the last, painful remnants of her struggle for maturity.

CHAPTER TWELVE

JEANNE was ticketed on a late morning flight to New York. But the British Airways ticket agent was very understanding when she explained that there was an emergency and she had to get home as soon as possible.

Actually, she thought as her plane lifted off, it was the truth. *She* was the emergency; her heart felt as if it were made of glass and might, at any moment, shatter.

There was a picture trapped in her mind: it was of Gray, as he had made love to her, his eyes dark with longing, his mouth taut with desire, his body poised above hers in that last moment before they had become one.

No matter how she tried, the picture would not go away. It was as if it were a loop of videotape projected against the background of her mind and everything else was played over it. It was there, on the window glass in the first-class cabin, on the cover of the glossy magazine offered to her by the flight attendant, on the dark of her closed eyelids when she lay her head back and tried to sleep.

Would it be there for the rest of her life? she wondered. Would that one moment in time, that one perfect moment, torment her forever?

Tears welled under her closed lashes, then trickled slowly down her cheeks. What was it Gray had said, that last terrible night at Caldwell House?

'I pick the woman, the time, and the place.'

And he had done just that, last night. But she had chosen, too: she had chosen the man she would always love. The memory of his kisses, of his passion, would be painful for a while, yes, but eventually would come the bitter-sweet joy of knowing that she had, at least, those remembrances.

The knowledge brought tranquillity, and Jeanne slept.

To her surprise, Seth was waiting at the gate at Kennedy Airport. How did you know I'd be on this flight? she almost said, but then she realised that Gray must have phoned British Airways, tracked her down, and telephoned New York.

That he still saw himself as responsible for her seemed, under the circumstances, almost laughable.

She put on a bright smile and went into her brother's arms. 'Hi,' she said, kissing his cheek. 'What a nice surprise—I didn't expect a welcoming committee.'

'You almost didn't get one. I had to juggle my morning appointments.' He glanced at her as he picked up her suitcase. 'Kind of sudden, this decision to come home, wasn't it?'

Jeanne flushed. 'No,' she said cautiously, 'not really. I had to come home eventually.' She cleared her throat as they reached the exit doors. 'What did Gray tell you?'

'Not much. Just that he'd finally managed to hire a permanent companion for his aunt, so he didn't need your services any more. And that you wanted to get back for some kind of audition.'

She nodded, relieved. 'Yes, that's right.'

Seth took her arm as they stepped out into the muggy New York evening. 'So what part are you up for?'

She looked at him. 'What?'

'The audition. What's it for?'

'Er—a commercial. A—er—a coffee commercial.'

'We were kind of surprised, Kristin and I,' he said as he hurried her across the roadway towards the car park. 'I mean, Gray's back in London, right? We thought you'd have spent a few days there, too. You know, see the sights, let him show you around.'

Jeanne shook her head as they reached the pavement. 'What for? I'd seen London when I was still with the tour group.'

'Well, yeah, but Gray could have——'

'And I've that audition coming up.'

'I know that, Jeannie. But——'

'Seth.' She swung around to face him. 'I have a life here, and it was time I came home and tended to it.'

'Look, you can't blame me for wishing my sister and my old buddy had fallen for each other.'

Jeanne stared at him. 'What?'

He smiled sheepishly. 'Hell, Jeanne, there's nothing so terrible in that. Gray's a good guy, and you——'

'You set me up, didn't you? That call you asked me to make to Graham Caldwell—that wasn't so he could check on me, it was because you hoped we'd—we'd ...'

He shrugged as he unlocked his car and tossed her luggage into the rear seat.

'Look, what's the difference? You and Gray didn't hit it off. That kind of thing happens. I just——'

A hot, unreasoning anger spread in her breast. 'You just have to stop interfering in my life,' she said. Her voice began to tremble; she took a deep breath before she dared go on. 'It's a dangerous game you were playing. There are—there are terrible risks.'

Seth's smile fled, and he stared at her. 'What is it, Jeannie? Did something——'

'I love you very much, Seth. And I know you love me, too. But from now on, it's hands off. Do you understand?'

The words were the most difficult she had ever said. She saw a quick flash of pain in her brother's eyes, but his next words told her the pain was for her, not for himself.

'Something *did* happen, didn't it?'

She hesitated. It would be easy to lie, she thought. She was a good actress, a better one than even she had realised. Hadn't the last weeks—and last night—proved it?

But lying was for children. Adults faced things head-on.

She drew a deep breath. 'Yes,' she said softly, 'something did. But I'm not going to discuss it,' she added, before he could speak. She stepped close to him and put her hand on his arm. 'Seth—I know you want to help. But you can't. This is my life, and I have to live it. Do you see?'

His eyes searched hers. 'Little Jeannie is really gone, isn't she?' he said after a moment. There was a terrible sadness in his voice.

She gave him a shaky smile. 'Yes,' she whispered, 'she's gone forever.' Her throat closed. She waited a moment, and then she swallowed. 'But the new me loves you just as much as the old.'

She saw the effort it took for him to smile at her in return, but finally he managed.

'You'd better,' he said. He gave her a long, hard look, and then he motioned her into the car. 'OK,' he said briskly, 'let's get moving. I've a wife at home who's dying to see you. She wanted to come to the airport with me, but I told her she was too pregnant to take out without warning the public.'

Jeanne laughed. 'I don't know how Kristin puts up with you, brother mine.'

Seth laughed, too. 'What choice does she have? She knows I'd never let her get away from me, even if she tried.'

Jeanne's smile faded as the car moved into the night. That was the truth, she thought; when you loved someone, you held on to them.

You didn't hand them an aeroplane ticket and send them away.

But then, Gray had never pretended to love her.

He had never pretended to anything. All that he'd wanted was to take her to bed.

She glanced at the dashboard clock. What was he doing now? she wondered. Whatever it was, she could only imagine his sense of relief that she was gone.

Her Greenwich Village flat was hot and airless. There'd been a water leak in the bathroom—the bath and floor were stained with rust. And insect life she preferred not to identify had set up housekeeping under the kitchen sink. Jeanne unpacked, then changed to old jeans and a frayed T-shirt and attacked the flat with detergent, hot water, and a dousing of insecticide. The job took the better part of the day. When she finished, she bathed, fell into bed, and slept until the next morning.

A job was next on the agenda. She put on a pair of sensible shoes and stalked the city streets, going from one restaurant to another, until she found an opening at a trendy little Italian place on the East Side. She worked from four in the afternoon until closing, which left her days free for auditions and study. It was an exhausting schedule, one that sent her tumbling gratefully into bed each night. There was no time to think, which was exactly what she wanted.

A few weeks later, she found herself serving dinner to two men whose faces seemed familiar.

Of course! They were a famous producing duo; she had tried out for their current play.

Jeanne said nothing. What would be the point? Neither man recognised her, of course. Eager young actresses were as easy to find in Manhattan as squirrels in Central Park. But as she poured them second cups of coffee, she couldn't help overhearing their conversation about finding a replacement for the girl who understudied the two female leads.

'Damned bad timing, if you ask me,' one of the men growled. 'Breaking her leg that way—who asked the foolish twit to go rock-climbing, anyway?' He stubbed his cigar into the ashtray. 'We'll just have to cross our fingers and pray neither Marge or Beverly comes down with anything worse than acne until we've a new understudy.'

'Until we've a new understudy who knows their lines, you mean. Some of those scenes are endless. It'll take a girl days to——'

'I know the lines,' Jeanne blurted. The men looked up, amused, and she flushed. 'I'm sorry. But I heard what you were saying.'

One of the men smiled. 'Don't tell us,' he said with exaggerated civility. 'You just happen to be an actress.'

Her flush deepened. 'Yes. And I know the play you're talking about. I auditioned for the second lead, so I know those lines. And I know most of the first lead, too. I read the play so often, you see, and...'

She fell silent. The men's faces were expressionless. Jeanne swallowed hard.

'I'm sorry. I shouldn't have...'

The men looked at each other, and then the one who'd been smoking the cigar dug in his pocket and pulled out a card.

'Show that at the stage door tomorrow morning.' His brows drew together. 'Not that I'm making any promises.'

Jeanne's heart leaped. 'Thank you,' she said. 'Thank you very much.'

To her amazement and delight, she got the job. She was paid union scale for sitting in the theatre every afternoon and evening, alternately hoping neither Marge or Bev, both of whom were sweet, likeable women, became ill—and praying that one of them would.

'Typical understudy paranoia,' Bev said cheerfully, reading Jeanne's face one evening when she'd arrived almost too late to make the curtain. 'You love us both, but, oh, how you wish one of us would get a whopping case of the flu!'

Jeanne laughed. 'Stay healthy,' she said. 'I'm content just to watch from the wings.'

Eventually, she was given a walk-on part, and then two lines in the second act.

The world was hers—at least, it should have been.

She had a real job in the theatre. She was learning more and more about her craft. And she had a beautiful little nephew; Kristin had been delivered of a chubby baby boy, just as the summer leaves began to turn to crimson and gold.

It was just that something strange had started happening to her.

Suddenly, each tall, dark-haired man in the street reminded her of Gray.

Each low black sports car looked like his; each male voice had a timbre that reminded her, at least for a heart-stopping second, of him.

She started dreaming about Gray; long, complex imaginings in which she saw him at a distance and tried to move towards him, only to find herself caught in a quagmire from which she never seemed to manage to escape. And, when she wasn't dreaming, she lay wide-eyed, wracked by insomnia, wondering where Gray was and what he was doing—and whether he ever, in quiet moments, thought of her.

'You have too much time on your hands,' she told her reflection firmly one evening. 'That's your trouble. After all, you aren't waiting on tables half the night any more.'

It seemed logical, and so Jeanne added things to her day: an aerobics workout early each morning. A jog around the Central Park reservoir. An afternoon dance class at the Y. And it helped—or she thought it did, until one evening at Kristin and Seth's Manhattan *pièd-á-terre*, when her carefully controlled existence suddenly fell apart.

She and Kristin were standing over the baby's crib, admiring the sleeping child.

'Isn't he wonderful?' Kristin whispered.

Jeanne nodded. 'He's a beautiful baby.'

Her sister-in-law's smile was radiant. 'That's because he looks like Seth,' she said softly, smoothing her son's hair back from his forehead. 'I can't tell you what it's like to look at that little face and know that he's ours, Seth's and mine, that our love created something so perfect and special.' She looked back at Jeanne and smiled self-consciously. 'Does that make any sense, or am I making new-mother noises?'

Jeanne nodded again. 'It makes absolute sense,' she said, and then, to her shock and horror, she burst into tears. She stared at Kristin, then put her hand to her mouth and turned away. 'Oh, God,' she whispered. 'Kristin, I'm sorry. Forgive me, please. I don't know what came over me just now.'

Kristin put her arm around Jeanne's shoulders and led her into the living-room.

'You haven't been yourself since you came back from England,' she said. 'I kept telling that to Seth, but he said you'd warned him to keep hands off.'

'I'll be all right. Really. I'm just—I'm working hard, you see, and...'

'It's Gray Caldwell, isn't it? Seth said you didn't care for him, but he was wrong, wasn't he?'

Jeanne nodded. 'Yes,' she whispered. 'But there's no sense talking about it.'

Kristin put her hands on Jeanne's shoulders. 'Are you pregnant?' she asked gently.

'Pregnant?' Jeanne gave a choked little laugh. 'No. No, I'm not pregnant. But that would be the final touch in this little melodrama, wouldn't it?'

'What is it, then?' Kristin led Jeanne to the sofa and the women sat. 'Jeannie,' she said softly, 'talk to me. Maybe I can help.'

Jeanne's eyes blurred with tears. 'No one can help,' she whispered. 'It's just a sad little story, Kristin, like—like a bad play.' She wiped the back of her hand across her nose. 'Girl meets boy, girl falls in love with boy—

boy waves goodbye.' Her eyes met those of her sister-in-law. 'Curtain down, houselights up. End of story.'

Kristin smiled. 'Hardly the end, if you're still crying over the guy months later. Does he know how you feel?'

'Does he...?' Jeanne laughed. 'No. I may be walking around with my heart on my sleeve now, but at least I managed to keep things under wraps while I was in England.' She rose and walked across the room to where she'd left her handbag. 'You see, Gray and I—we played this sophisticated little game of—of seduction,' she said, burrowing in the bag for her handkerchief. She put it to her nose and blew. 'One step forward, two steps back. It's hard to explain...'

Kristin sighed. 'You don't have to explain. It wasn't all smooth sailing for your brother and me, remember?'

Jeanne shook her head. 'But that was different. Seth loved you. There was never any doubt about that.'

'*I* doubted it. I was convinced he'd just wanted a casual affair. And I ran away before he could tell me the truth.'

Jeanne sighed and fell into the chair across from Kristin. 'I know you mean well,' she said. 'But there aren't any parallels. Gray doesn't love me. He never did, not even for a minute.'

'Are you sure? Sometimes we don't hear everything we——'

'He doesn't even like me very much, if you want to know the truth.' Colour rose in Jeanne's face. 'He wanted me. But that was—it was...'

'Sex,' Kristin said gently. 'But sex is a part of love, Jeanne. Maybe——'

'Do you know what I was doing at Caldwell House?' Jeanne drew a breath. 'I wasn't there because his aunt needed a companion. I was there to keep the local belles from cluttering the parlour.' Kristin's brows rose, and Jeanne nodded. 'It's true. Gray Caldwell is a very contented bachelor. He has no interest in giving up the good life for anyone.' Her mouth trembled. 'Especially not for me.'

'Yes, but if you're this unhappy——'

'He doesn't know I'm unhappy. He thinks things ended just the way both of us wanted.'

'Well, then, maybe you should get in touch with the man. Tell him——'

Jeanne rose to her feet. 'Haven't you heard a thing I said? Gray and I didn't have a love-affair. We just—we just...'

'Jeanne, dear.'

'As far as Gray knows, we were two people who—who took pleasure in each other and then went on with their lives.'

'So you left London with your pride intact.'

'Exactly.'

Kristin smiled gently. 'And your heart in a hundred pieces.'

Jeanne blew her nose again. 'That wasn't Gray's fault,' she said wearily. 'I was the one who fell in love, not he.' She looked at Kristin and sighed. 'It's a long, complicated story. But the bottom line is that I made a mess of things, and now I have to put that mess behind me and—and——'

'Gray may be coming to New York.'

Jeanne's heart knocked against her ribs. 'Did Seth——? I'll never forgive my brother if——'

'Seth had nothing to do with it. Gray has business here.' She hesitated. 'We'll have him to dinner or something, when he comes. Maybe——'

'No!' Jeanne put her hand to her breast. 'No,' she repeated. 'I don't want to see him. Not ever.'

'Jeanne——'

'Promise me you won't tell any of this to Seth.' Jeanne's eyes sought those of her sister-in-law. 'Kristin? Promise me.'

Kristin sighed. 'If that's what you want.'

'It is,' Jeanne said positively. 'I know my brother. He'd only try to help—he'd do something or say something or...' She shook her head. 'You won't tell Seth?'

Kristin smiled. 'Trust me.'

Autumn turned to winter. Jeanne was uncomfortable at first, half expecting Seth to say something about her abortive love-affair. But he didn't, and after a while she relaxed.

Apparently, Kristin had kept her promise.

She worried, too, about Gray's being in New York. But, as the weeks passed without his name being mentioned, she decided his plans had changed.

The play she'd been in closed finally. The last performance was a Wednesday matinée, played to a half-empty house. Jeanne's lines were delivered to another actor at stage centre; she said them almost without thinking, they were so familiar by then—and suddenly she felt the hair rise on the back of her neck.

It was as if there were an unknown presence in the darkened theatre. She stumbled over her last words, and her gaze went past the actor and across the footlights.

She could see the audience, or what there was of it. They were the same shadowy figures as always. There was nothing unusual about that; whatever it was she'd sensed had come from the rear of the theatre, from somewhere beyond the last aisle.

The curtain rang down, then rose again to desultory applause. The houselights came up, the cast came on for bows, and Jeanne scanned the lit auditorium. But there was nothing—and no one—unusual to be seen.

'It was probably the ghost of the last play that folded and died in this place,' one of the other girls said, laughing as she heard Jeanne's story. She scrubbed the last of her make-up from her face, fluffed her hair, and rose from their shared dressing-table. 'See you on the unemployment line tomorrow.'

Jeanne smiled as she put on her coat and buttoned it against the winter evening.

It was true. Tomorrow, she'd be back pounding the pavement. But tonight would be pleasant: Seth and

Kristin were in town with the baby, they had some sort of business dinner to attend, and they'd asked her to baby-sit.

'I have to meet Seth at five-thirty,' Kristin had said. 'You will be on time, won't you?'

'Am I ever late for an engagement with my nephew?' Jeanne had answered, and the two women had laughed.

Promptly at five, she rang the doorbell at their flat. Kristin answered; to Jeanne's surprise, the baby, dressed for the street, was in her arms.

'Change of plans,' she sang out. 'Seth wants to show us both off to some out-of-town bigwig. I'm taking the baby with me.'

Jeanne stared at her. 'To drinks and dinner?'

Her sister-in-law shrugged. 'Crazy, isn't it? But we're dining in their suite at the Waldorf; I told Seth to arrange for a crib and all the rest . . . Just look at the time! Sorry, dear, I've got to fly.'

'Kristin—are you sure you——?'

'There's cold ham in the fridge, and cheese. Help yourself. We'll chat later.'

'But I'm not going to stay if you——'

Kristin kissed her cheek as she brushed past her to the elevator. 'Of course you will. We haven't seen you in ages; we're looking forward to it. We won't be late, Jeannie. Ta-ra.'

The elevator doors opened, then closed. Jeanne stood staring at the empty hall, and then she laughed and shut the apartment door.

Parenthood had done strange things to her brother and his wife. Seth had never struck her as the sort who'd trot out a fistful of baby pictures for strangers and yet here he was, showing off his infant son to some out-of-town client.

Well, who could blame him? The baby was beautiful. He was . . .

The peal of the doorbell caught her in mid-stride. Kristin had forgotten something—nappies or formula or one of the baby's toys. She smiled as she unlocked the door. Maybe she'd simply come to her senses and decided not to oblige her daft husband by dragging their son off to dinner at the...

The smile fell from her face as she swung open the door. There, framed in the doorway, wearing an expression of shock that surely matched her own, was Gray.

Her first instinct was simply to slam the door in his face. But what would be the sense to that? Gray would still be standing just on the other side of it, he wouldn't vanish in a puff of smoke.

Say something, she thought furiously, but it was he who recovered first.

'What are you doing here?'

His voice was cold and angry. The sound of it gave her the courage she had, a moment ago, lacked.

'I think that's *my* question, don't you?' How calm and cool she sounded; no one would know her pulse was racing. He looked—he looked so handsome. And so tired. There were shadows under his eyes, lines around his mouth.

'I was invited to dinner.' His eyes narrowed. 'Don't tell me you've been invited, too.'

Jeanne shook her head. 'No, of course not.' She stared at him. 'You must have got the day wrong. Seth and Kristin are out.'

'It's Wednesday, isn't it? The nineteenth?' He frowned and stepped past her into the entry foyer. 'What do you mean, they're out?'

Jeanne let go of the door. It swung shut with a resounding thump. 'Just what I said. They've gone out to dinner. Are you sure Seth said——?'

'Kristin invited me. I phoned to say I was in town, and she said, why didn't we surprise Seth? "Come to dinner Wednesday," she said. "Come early, at five-fifteen, so you get here before he does."' His frown deepened. 'Why are you looking at me that way?'

The breath puffed from Jeanne's lungs. 'Kristin,' she said softly. 'Kristin did this.'

'I just said she did. She asked me to dinner.'

Jeanne sighed. 'She asked me to baby-sit. She told me to be here at five promptly—and then, when I showed up, she marched out the door with the weirdest story.' Her voice trailed away. After a moment, she sighed again. 'Look, this is all my fault. I'm sorry you've been put to any trouble. I'll tell them you were here, and...'

Gray looked at her. 'Your fault? How?'

She swallowed. 'I—I said some things to Kristin that...' Their eyes met, and vertigo swept over her. She turned away quickly and folded her arms over her breasts. 'My family has this habit of interfering in my life,' she said softly. 'I'm sorry.'

Footsteps sounded behind her. She held her breath, waiting for his hands to clasp her shoulders, but they didn't. After a moment, he spoke.

'How have you been, Jeanne?'

His voice was low. The sound of it sent a tremor down her spine. 'Fine,' she said quickly. 'And you?'

There was a pause before he answered. 'Fine. Just fine. Busy, of course.'

She nodded. 'Yes, me, too. How—how's Abigail?'

He laughed softly. 'She's taken up croquet. She says it's a sport for old women, but when you see her whack that mallet, you have to wince for the poor ball.'

Jeanne smiled. 'I can imagine.' Silence fell between them. 'I've been working. In a play. A real part.'

'Yes. I know. Seth mentioned it.'

'It closed today.'

'Yes.'

She heard the shift of his weight. The hair rose on her nape; she knew he had moved closer to her, and suddenly she knew something else, as well.

'Were you—were you in the theatre this afternoon?' she whispered.

Gray sighed. 'Yeah. I didn't manage to catch the whole play. But I saw you in the second act—you were wonderful.'

She closed her eyes and hugged herself more closely. 'I knew someone was there,' she said. 'I should have known—no one else would have made me feel...' Her lips clamped together. What was she doing? Another minute and she was going to make a fool of herself, she was going to say and do stupid things she would never forgive herself for. She drew in her breath, then turned slowly to face him. 'I'm sorry you've had this trip for nothing. I'll tell Seth to phone you in——'

'Jeannie.'

The whispered word hung in the silence. Jeanne raised her eyes slowly to Gray's face, and her breath caught. He was watching her through eyes as dark as the pain in her heart.

'Jeannie,' he said again. She stiffened as he reached out and touched her face. His hands were cool with the chill of the January night. 'Why did you run away from me?'

'I didn't run,' she said quickly. She swallowed. 'I mean—what was the point in staying? The morning would have been—it would have been hard for both of us. Uncomfortable. You——'

'Yes.' His voice was a whisper. 'It would have been agony.'

She blinked as tears rose in her eyes. Don't cry, she told herself fiercely. Don't cry!

'Well, then,' she said. 'You see? That's why I——'

His hands slipped into her hair and tilted her face up. 'It would have been agony to watch you leave me. But I knew there was no way to stop you, Jeannie. I cared too much to try and deny you your freedom.'

She stared at him, suddenly mute.

Gray moved closer to her. 'But I would have made love to you again.' His gaze fell to her parted lips. '

would have kissed you, and tasted you, and made you cry out my name.'

Jeanne swayed, and his hands slid to her shoulders and held her tightly.

'Just—just tell me you're happy now.' His eyes met hers. 'Tell me you're happy, and I'll—I'll let you go. I'll turn away and leave, and——'

'No!' The cry was torn from her heart. Her hands lifted slowly; she lay them flat against Gray's chest. 'Don't—don't go. Not yet. Not until you've—you've——'

He groaned as he gathered her into his arms and kissed her. It was a kiss more sweet than any they had ever shared. There was desire in his kiss, and need, and something more.

Something more. Something that made Jeanne tremble. Something...

The tears Jeanne had tried to contain spilled down her cheeks. 'Oh, Gray,' she whispered.

'I know you don't want anybody worrying about you. Or interfering in your life.' His hands slid to her jaw and framed her face. 'Or loving you, dammit! But I can't help what I feel. I promised myself I would never tell you, and I didn't. Not at Caldwell House, not that night when we made love, not in all the empty weeks and months since, but I must tell you now, Jeannie. I love you. I'll always love you. Do you hear me?'

The words, the wonderful words she had dreamed of, seemed impossible to believe. She stared at him until he kissed her again, a slow kiss that left her breathless.

'I think I loved you almost from the beginning,' he whispered. 'But you made me so damned angry—I kept imagining the men you'd been with——'

She smiled. 'There was no one. No one but you. I wanted to tell you—I almost did. But at first I didn't think you'd believe me. And then I—I was afraid to. I felt so vulnerable, you see, because I'd fallen so desperately in love with you.'

They stared at each other. 'Do you mean it?' Gray asked hoarsely. She nodded, and his expression grew fierce. 'Then why didn't you tell me? Why did you leave me? Why——?'

'I thought—you said all those things about the importance of being free——'

He groaned. 'I was talking about *you*, Jeannie, not me. I was trying to tell you I understood your need to live your own life.' His mouth twisted. 'But it was a damned lie. I didn't want you to be free; I wanted you to be mine. For the rest of our lives. I wanted to tell you that, after we'd made love. But you said——'

Jeanne put her hand to his cheek. 'How terribly we misunderstood each other,' she said softly. 'I was trying to keep you from feeling responsible for what had happened.'

'And I was trying to grant you the freedom I thought you wanted.'

Gray's arms closed around her, and he held her to him. After a long while, Jeanne drew back in his arms and they smiled at each other.

'So,' Jeanne said softly, 'Kristin invited you here tonight, hmm?'

Gray began to laugh. 'At five-fifteen. Not a minute earlier, she insisted. And not a minute later.'

Jeanne sighed. 'She made the whole thing up, I suppose. The business dinner—all of it. There's nothing I can do with them,' she said. 'I have the most interfering family in the world, and they're never going to change.'

His mouth moved gently along her temple, to her cheek. Her head fell back, and his kisses brushed lightly along her throat.

'All the more reason to spend our honeymoon on some deserted island, darling.' His voice was husky. 'Can you survive a month alone with no one but me, do you think?'

Jeanne clasped his face between her hands and brought his mouth to hers. 'Only if we start practising now,' she whispered.

A long time later, the phone rang and rang, then finally went silent. Jeanne stirred in Gray's arms.

'We should answer that,' she said.

He smiled and kissed her. 'It's probably Seth.'

Jeanne smiled, too. 'And Kristin. I suppose they want to know what happened.'

Gray's eyes darkened as he drew Jeanne to him. 'Shall we answer the phone and tell them?'

Jeanne laughed softly as the phone rang again. 'Later,' she said.

'Much later,' Gray agreed.

After a while, the phone stopped ringing.

HARLEQUIN
Romance®

and WEDDINGS go together—
especially in June!
So don't miss next month's title in

THE BRIDAL COLLECTION

LOVE YOUR ENEMY
by Ellen James

THE BRIDE led the anti-Jarrett forces.
THE GROOM was Jarrett!
THE WEDDING? An Attraction of Opposites!

Available this month in
THE BRIDAL COLLECTION

FREE GIFT OFFER

To receive your free gift, send us the specified number of proofs-of-purchase from any specially marked Free Gift Offer Harlequin or Silhouette book with the Free Gift Certificate properly completed, plus a check or money order (do not send cash) to cover postage and handling payable to Harlequin/Silhouette Free Gift Promotion Offer. We will send you the specified gift.

FREE GIFT CERTIFICATE

ITEM	A. GOLD TONE EARRINGS	B. GOLD TONE BRACELET	C. GOLD TONE NECKLACE
# of proofs-of-purchase required	3	6	9
Postage and Handling	$1.75	$2.25	$2.75
Check one	☐	☐	☐

Name: _____

Address: _____

City: _____ State: _____ Zip Code: _____

Mail this certificate, specified number of proofs-of-purchase and a check or money order for postage and handling to: HARLEQUIN/SILHOUETTE FREE GIFT OFFER 1992, P.O. Box 9057, Buffalo, NY 14269-9057. Requests must be received by July 31, 1992.

PLUS—Every time you submit a completed certificate with the correct number of proofs-of-purchase, you are automatically entered in our MILLION DOLLAR SWEEPSTAKES! No purchase or obligation necessary to enter. See below for alternate means of entry and how to obtain complete sweepstakes rules.

MILLION DOLLAR SWEEPSTAKES
NO PURCHASE OR OBLIGATION NECESSARY TO ENTER

To enter, hand-print (mechanical reproductions are not acceptable) your name and address on a 3"×5" card and mail to Million Dollar Sweepstakes 6097, c/o either P.O. Box 9056, Buffalo, NY 14269-9056 or P.O. Box 621, Fort Erie, Ontario L2A 5X3. Limit: one entry per envelope. Entries must be sent via 1st-class mail. For eligibility, entries must be received no later than March 31, 1994. No liability is assumed for printing errors, lost, late or misdirected entries.

Sweepstakes is open to persons 18 years of age or older. All applicable laws and regulations apply. Sweepstakes offer void wherever prohibited by law. Prizewinners will be determined no later than May 1994. Chances of winning are determined by the number of entries distributed and received. For a copy of the Official Rules governing this sweepstakes offer, send a self-addressed, stamped envelope (WA residents need not affix return postage) to: Million Dollar Sweepstakes Rules, P.O. Box 4733, Blair, NE 68009.

✂ HP2U

ONE PROOF-OF-PURCHASE

To collect your fabulous FREE GIFT you must include the necessary FREE GIFT proofs-of-purchase with a properly completed offer certificate.

(See inside back cover for offer details)

Coming Next Month

Available in June wherever paperback books are sold, or through Harlequin Reader Service:

In the U.S.
P.O. Box 1397
Buffalo, NY
14240-1397

In Canada
P.O. Box 603
Fort Erie, Ontario
L2A 5X3

Summer Reading
At Its Best

In July, Harlequin and Silhouette bring readers the Big Summer Read Program. Heat up your summer with these four exciting new novels by top Harlequin and Silhouette authors.

SOMEWHERE IN TIME by Barbara Bretton
YESTERDAY COMES TOMORROW by Rebecca Flanders
A DAY IN APRIL by Mary Lynn Baxter
LOVE CHILD by Patricia Coughlin

From time travel to fame and fortune, this program offers something for everyone.

Available at your favorite retail outlet.

BSR

GREAT TEMPTRESSES WORD SEARCH CONTEST

Harlequin wants to give romance readers the chance to receive a fabulous GE SPACEMAKER TV, ABSOLUTELY FREE, just for entering our *Great Temptresses* Word Search Contest. To qualify, complete the word search puzzle below and send it to us so that we receive it by June 26, 1992. Ten entries chosen by random draw will receive a GE SPACEMAKER TV, complete with 6.5" B & W screen, a swivel bracket for easy hanging and built-in AM/FM radio!!!

YOU COULD GET A FREE GE SPACEMAKER TV, JUST FOR PLAYING!

```
B E T T Y G R A B L E L R S D
T K E I R A H A T A M N C N E
L Y M E L L E S S M E H L R E
L E A S A L O M E B E E E C O
A C D O O W A N W H Q L O U R
C E O E B N Z L E A R E P J N
A F N G R H I R A L O N A B O
B X N Z A X A P M I N O T T M
N Y A C G Z D O R L J F R B N
E S I V A D E T T E B T A I Y
R M O D T S U V C D J R V O L
U R E A E P Q W H H L O Q Y I
A M J C R W A O T S E Y H I R
L A D Y G O D I V A B R X C A
S S C A R L E T T O H A R A M
```

MARILYN MONROE	SALOME
DELILAH	BETTE DAVIS
GRETA GARBO	CLEOPATRA
MADONNA	LAUREN BACALL
MATA HARI	BETTY GRABLE
CHER	SCHEHERAZADE
HELEN OF TROY	MAE WEST
LADY GODIVA	SCARLETT O'HARA

HOW TO ENTER

All the names listed are hidden in the word puzzle grid. You can find them by reading the letters forward, backward, up and down, or diagonally. When you find a word, circle it or put a line through it. Then fill in your name and address in the space provided, put this page in an envelope, and mail it today to:

H1MAY

Harlequin *Great Temptresses* Word Search Contest
Harlequin Reader Service®
P.O. Box 9071
Buffalo, NY 14269-9071

NAME _____

ADDRESS _____

_____

CITY _____ STATE _____ ZIP CODE _____

H1MAY

Ten (10) winners will be selected from all property completed entries in a random drawing from all entries on or about July 1, 1992. Odds of winning are dependent upon the number of entries received. Winners will be notified by mail. Decisions of the judges are final. Open to all residents of the U.S., 18 years or older, except employees and families of Torstar Corporation, its affiliates and subsidiaries. Winners consent to the use of their name, photograph or likeness for advertising and publicity in conjunction with this and similar promotions without additional compensation.